Nanette Brinson

Also by Dennis McKay

Novels:
Fallow's Field (2007)
Once Upon Wisconsin (2009)
A Boy From Bethesda (2013)
The Shaman and the Stranger (2015)
The Accidental Philanderer (2015)
A Girl From Bethesda (2017)
Summer of Tess (2018)
Bethany Blue (2019)
In Search of Cloud People (2020)
Life and Times of Scuffy Lomax (2020)
LA Easy (2021)

Nonfiction:
Terrapin Tales, with coauthor Scott McBrien (2016)

Nanette Brinson

Dennis McKay

NANETTE BRINSON

iUniverse books may be ordered through booksellers or by contacting:

iUniverse
1663 Liberty Drive
Bloomington, IN 47403
www.iuniverse.com
844-349-9409

Because of the dynamic nature of the Internet, any web addresses or links contained in this book may have changed since publication and may no longer be valid. The views expressed in this work are solely those of the author and do not necessarily reflect the views of the publisher, and the publisher hereby disclaims any responsibility for them.

Any people depicted in stock imagery provided by Getty Images are models, and such images are being used for illustrative purposes only. Certain stock imagery © Getty Images.

Book cover design by Megan Belford

ISBN: 978-1-6632-4046-0 (sc)
ISBN: 978-1-6632-4045-3 (e)

Library of Congress Control Number: 2022914088

Print information available on the last page.

iUniverse rev. date: 08/23/2022

CHAPTER 1

April 2010

H ER FATHER HAD TOLD HER on her sixteenth birthday, "Nanette, you were a beauty the day you were born and will be 'til the day you depart this earth." But her beauty had been, in some ways, her defining characteristic that had taken her life into a negative void. Before she completed college, she married a grad student she had met in the theater, where she played Stella in *A Streetcar Named Desire*, and he was the lighting operator.

Nanette had seriously considered a career as an actor before Roger stormed into her life. It had been a whirlwind romance with barely time to understand what she had gotten herself into. He was her first serious relationship, her first time intimate, her first time where someone came before the stage.

As she turned off the Capital Beltway and onto the exit ramp for I-95 South—leaving Bethesda–Chevy Chase in her rearview mirror—an image emerged through the staggered distance of memories, evoking the thrill of that first time performing on stage in eighth grade, playing Emily Gibbs in *Our Town*. Nanette had penetrated her character with a creative joy that was so new and exhilarating. And never would she forget the turning-point line, when Emily asked if anyone truly understood the value of life as they live it.

Well, Nanette thought, *I didn't before Roger passed.* But now, it would be different. After thirty-eight years of marriage and one grown son—Connor, living in Auckland, New Zealand, as a research marine biologist—Nanette was ready to open herself up to new possibilities.

In her mother's day, it would have been unheard of for a widow in her sixtieth year to sell her home and all its furnishings (through a consignment shop), leave her roots, and buy a fully furnished house that she had seen only through an online virtual tour—in Florida, no less—and head out on her own for the unknown. Maybe meet a man, someone who was a free-spirited sort without a lot of rules, unlike her husband.

In researching her new neighborhood, Nanette discovered that the Pleasantville Theater Company had upcoming auditions for *The Glass Menagerie*, another Tennessee Williams classic; Nanette had seen the film version years ago.

After successfully merging onto the busy interstate crammed with an endless stream of noisy, gear-grinding trucks and whizzing cars, she said aloud, "Let's not get ahead of ourselves."

She had said that to herself repeatedly after Roger's heart attack, which took him away within a matter of minutes. He was in the middle of mowing the yard when Mr. Death came a-calling. The loss of her husband brought on mixed feelings: a sense of vulnerability, no longer having Roger to manage their financial affairs, the yard, and any problems in the house that he took care of or called someone to fix. But on the other hand, Nanette felt a sense of freedom, as though she had escaped from a stifling environment—a world where her voice was heard but rarely listened to.

But after she sold Roger's real estate business and became financially independent, an inner calm came over Nanette, a sense of independence that she had not felt since college. Six months after her husband's death, here she was.

By midafternoon, Nanette had checked in at a four-story oceanfront hotel in Wrightsville Beach, North Carolina. She had purchased a bottle of Chablis for just this moment, and now, she took a seat on her balcony.

The faint chime of bells broke the moment. She found her cell phone on the countertop of the efficiency kitchen and saw her son's name on the screen. "Connor," she said as she returned to the balcony, "hello there."

"How's the trip going, Mom?"

"I am sitting on the third-floor balcony of my room at the Surf's Suites in North Carolina, with a view of the Atlantic Ocean, a gentle ocean breeze in my face, and … a glass of Chablis in hand."

"Wish I could have been there to assist you in all this," Connor said.

"You have your life to live," Nanette said with all the enthusiasm she could muster, for truth be told, it would have been comforting if Connor had been able to stick around after Roger's funeral, but he had been in the middle of applying for a research grant from the University of Auckland, which he eventually received, and only stayed for the funeral and the day after.

"How is the research going?" Nanette asked.

"My team and I are going out to sea next week to take plankton samples—I won't bother you with the details, but suffice it to say, I'm excited about our prospects." Connor went on to mention that he had begun dating a woman in his field. "She is working on her doctorate at the University of Auckland."

"Really," Nanette said in a tone that said, *Tell me more.*

"I'll keep you posted, Mom," Connor said through a laugh.

After talking with her son, Nanette sat back and took a swallow of her wine. The crisp taste had an immediate unwinding effect, as though her body exhaled in one big breath. Out on the wide beach, a smattering of people—young, mostly—lounged on blankets and beach chairs. A couple of surfers in wetsuits were trying to surf, but the waves were rather small. Gulls and terns were swooping over the shoreline, an occasional faint squawk echoing into the air before dying out.

Nanette was truly happy for Connor; he had worked hard to get to this point in his career. After graduating college in the States, he traveled the world for six months and stayed in New Zealand, where he met a girl. The relationship didn't last, but he stayed and received his PhD at the University of Auckland. It seemed Nanette's son had found a permanent residence far from home, now nearly ten years later.

Of course, she wished he lived closer to her, but it had facilitated her picking up and heading south. If Connor had been living nearby, she would have stayed put. But with nothing to keep her next door to the nation's capital in suburban Maryland, where she had spent all her life, save four years at a small liberal arts college in western Pennsylvania, an urge to start over grew stronger and stronger until she decided to move outside her comfort zone.

She finished her glass of wine and lifted the bottle of Chablis with her left hand. As Nanette poured her refill, she noticed her rose-gold wedding band. She worked the band off her finger, circumscribed by a thin white line. It reminded her of a brand.

When she had first laid eyes on it, she thought it ever so lovely. Roger had taken Nanette to the jeweler, and they looked over wedding bands with intricate overlays and cluster settings of small stones, but she liked the simple beauty and clean look of gold. Though it had held up well with only some minor tarnishing, it now represented something that she no longer felt a part of, no longer was a part of—marriage. If she was truly changing her life, then she needed to do one more thing.

She took a fortifying swallow of her wine and got up and headed for the door.

At the edge of the Atlantic, the waves lapped on shore, stopping short of the flip-flops Nanette had changed into. She positioned the wedding band between her thumb and forefinger and flicked it into the water, disappearing into the briny sea.

As Nanette turned and headed back to her room and the awaiting second glass of wine, she felt some kind of knowledge pass over her that was more visceral than knowing, but right then and there, a strange, happy confidence came over her—Nanette Brinson could do whatever she wanted.

On the afternoon of her third day on the road—Nanette had spent her second night at a Comfort Inn outside Savannah—she pulled into the parking lot of her realtor in Pleasantville, a quaint little place thirty miles south of The Villages, the largest retirement community in the world, which she had considered as a destination.

She had talked with friends of friends who lived in The Villages and decided against it—too big and with too many rules—although she was told she would never be lonely in The Villages. "There's something for everyone," was mentioned more than once. But Pleasantville had a local theater and with enough shops and conveniences nearby; it seemed like the right fit—not too big but big enough.

At the reception desk, Nanette identified herself, and before she could take a seat, an elderly gentleman in khaki slacks and a bright orange polo shirt appeared. "Nanette, you made it," he said in a welcoming baritone that brought to mind an announcer on a game show—*Come on down.*

Nanette recognized the voice as that of her realtor. He was tall—six foot four or so—with a long, lived-in face that was deeply tanned and lined. He looked to be a spry-looking eighty, a tennis player, possibly.

"Ed Feldman, here," he said as he offered his hand to Nanette, which she shook. Ed dangled keys on a chain. "I bet you are anxious to get into your new home." He reached behind the reception desk, clutched a bunch of pamphlets and brochures, and lifted his chin toward the door.

Nanette followed Ed's sleek black Mercedes through the middle of town. Both sides of the street were lined with brick sidewalks, old-fashioned wrought-iron streetlamps between walk and street, one- and two-story buildings, a few with window boxes teeming with colorful flowers. They passed the town square, dotted with palm trees, green vegetation in various geometric patterns, and a bandstand dressed by an octagonal slate roof. Pleasantville gave off the vibe of an upscale version of small-town America.

Through town and a few turns, she followed Ed onto a cul-de-sac and the asphalt driveway of a bungalow. The lawn was neatly trimmed, and a dogwood and red maple tree were on each side of a lazy-L-shaped, exposed aggregate walkway that led to the front door.

She took in the exterior of her new home, which looked more or less like what she had expected from her virtual tour: a one-story with a one-car garage and modest front porch—more of a stoop, actually—a low gabled roof, and pale-yellow vinyl siding with white trim that provided a cozy feel. *This is it,* Nanette thought as she got out of the car and exhaled.

After Ed departed, Nanette went back over the notes she had taken as he had explained where the water shut-off valve was and the power box—now these were her responsibility, all the things Roger would have handled and understood.

The house was sixteen years old, and Nanette was the second owner. Ed had told her that the first owners had been a retired couple, now in their nineties, who had moved to assisted living. "The previous owners took good care of this house, and you shouldn't have any major problems," Ed had told her. "But just in case, here is the card of a handyman who also is a resident of Pleasantville." He had gone on to say that the handyman only worked in Pleasantville and was retired and very reasonable. "He says he likes to fix things, and it's a way to meet neighbors."

The card listed Devin McCortland, CE, who did electrical, plumbing, carpentry, and more. Nanette thought the name intriguing. *Devin McCortland* didn't sound like a typical handyman name. And the fact that he was a civil engineer validated that assumption.

She placed the card in a kitchen drawer and decided to walk around her new home and begin the absorption process. The kitchen had granite countertops, traditional cabinets with bead-board design, a bench breakfast nook, and an island bar with three high-back stools. It adjoined a dining space with a round table and four chairs, which flowed into a living room, where the furnishings had a comfy feel, with a cushy sofa, a pair of oversized cozy chairs, a ship's table, and hardwood floor with a braided rug.

Off the front foyer was a guest bedroom with a queen-size bed covered by a chenille bedspread, a private bathroom and shower, and a double-wide window with a view of the front yard. On the other side of the foyer were an office setup with an oak desk and high-back leather office chair, a powder room, and the laundry space that led to the garage.

As she walked about, Nanette let not only the house but her new life sink into her bones in an attempt to establish a comfort level. From the living room, Nanette could access the master bedroom—that had been the clincher for her. It had a king-size bed with a grand headboard with vertical slats, sloped top rail, and octagonal bed posts. There was also a spacious shower and whirlpool bath in the bathroom and a walk-in closet.

A sliding glass door between the kitchen and living room opened to the flagstone patio, which faced a moderate-sized backyard with a raised vegetable bed—Ed had mentioned that the handyman built it—and a three-foot rail fence bordering the neighbor's yard. There was also an A-frame shed stocked with a gas-powered lawn mower and gardening tools and adorned by red impatiens in window boxes on the side and in front that added a homey touch. On the side of the shed was a bike rack with a woman's and a man's bicycles, each with a basket behind the seat. They reminded Nanette of bikes from her childhood, with wide handlebars and sturdy frames.

Nanette stood on the patio, taking it all in. Yes, it was all nice and welcoming, but a sense of loneliness hung over her. And compounding that loneliness was her feeling of being an interloper in someone else's home, which had a faint scent of other people, older people. She was in the home of strangers and all their belongings, on her own, with no husband to take care of things, no friends or family nearby. She was starting from square one, and now she faced the rest of her life. Whatever had she been thinking?

She missed her friends and the comfort of her old life, where she had a routine that she was used to. After Roger's funeral, Connor tried to convince his mother to visit him in New Zealand. "And if you like it, you could stay with me until you find your own place."

At the time, Nanette immediately rejected the thought of moving halfway across the world, but now, though it still seemed unlikely, it was, at least, something to consider if Florida did not work out.

CHAPTER 2

AS HE DEPARTED THE LUMBERYARD, Devin's mind drifted back, once again, to earlier in the day when he had first seen her. He had been in his pickup, en route to the lumberyard to pick up materials for a job, when he saw Ed Feldman escorting a woman into a recently sold bungalow. As he slowed to get a better look, a surge, like an awakening, stormed through him. It was like hearing a great song for the first time. She was ever so lovely and with a certain vulnerability, as though her life had taken a sudden turn.

As Devin passed, he watched from his rearview mirror as Ed opened the front door, and she entered. She wore a short-sleeved blouse and an A-line skirt that exposed shapely calves. But it was her face that had caught Devin's eye from the first. Enchanting, it was—the mouth full and inviting, prominent cheekbones, and a finely turned nosed. But besides her beauty and desirableness, Devin was drawn by her expressive yet subdued countenance, like an actor in character, as though she were in search of *something*—or possibly someone.

He guessed she was single, possibly a widow, a youthful-looking woman. He bet she was older than her appearance, for he knew the signs beyond the outer exterior: a stance and concentrated expression that registered a specific time of development—in her case, the mid-1950s to early '60s. He knew this because folks were always surprised when he told them he was sixty-four.

"You could pass for fifty or even younger," a woman for whom he'd recently fixed a leaky faucet told him.

So, Devin thought, *how to meet this most intriguing of women.* He knew it was crazy to have fallen for someone he only passed by for a five-second look-see, but there it was—the undeniable. He could wait for a maintenance call, but that might take years. Devin had never done a repair to that house, but he had built a raised garden bed a few years back and, more recently, had laid a flagstone patio before the house went on the market. The place was in good condition.

Or he could contact Ed Feldman and get the lowdown. But Devin didn't want to bring Ed into it. He was a bit too nosy for Devin's taste, though Devin was grateful that Ed handed out his business card to every new client who bought a home in the neighborhood.

No, he would wait a couple of days to let her get situated and then knock on her door, introduce himself as the local handyman, and see where it led. That way, in case she was involved or married, he could walk away unscathed.

CHAPTER 3

A FTER A RESTLESS FIRST NIGHT'S sleep, Nanette decided to take a bike ride around the neighborhood. She found a pump in the shed and pumped air into the tires of the woman's bike.

She walked the bike out to the street, slid her leg through the step-through frame, and sat on the seat. Nanette hadn't ridden in years, but it all came back as she peddled up the street, taking in the warm breeze. Each home was well maintained, and the yards, like hers, were neat and trim. She saw an older man tending to his garden bed of spiny plants and colorful flowers, and she passed men jogging in shorts and T-shirts and a couple walking, with *good mornings* exchanged. There was something too orderly about this scene unfolding before her.

Nanette told herself to give it all a chance—change was necessary to move on with her life—to become adaptable, and to look on the bright side. She was in a warm climate, which she loved; no more snow and sleet to worry about in winter, which she hated.

The bike was easy to peddle and reasonably comfortable. She sat erect, hands on the wide handlebars, just like her childhood bike. On Nanette's fifth birthday, she had received her first bike, a Schwinn that she first rode with training wheels. She scooted around her street, Fairglen Lane, in Bethesda, Maryland, and later, when the training wheels came off, the Bradley Boulevard Apartments, Nanette's first home, just a block away. She was the younger of two girls, three years apart.

For as long as she could remember, Nanette had been considered the family beauty. Her sister was attractive, but it became clear early on that Nanette was the apple of her father's eye. He nicknamed her

Nangorgeous, which Nanette basked in, but at the same time, she felt the displeasure of her older sister, Caroline.

By eighth grade at North Bethesda Junior High, Nanette was nearly fully formed. Her breasts were full and firm, and her face lost the childish appearance as the profile of a young woman emerged. Boys began showing interest, and her first date was to a Valentine's Day dance at the school gym. The boy, whose name Nanette could no longer remember, was shorter than Nanette. His squeaky, crackling voice only added to the disparity, as Nanette's had taken on a throaty, raspy timbre that gave the impression of an older girl.

When the quarterback on the high school team, who had asked Caroline out to a movie, arrived at the house, Nanette answered the door. His eyes lit up at the sight of her, a confident smile emerging. "Well, well," he said smoothly, "I didn't expect Ingrid Bergman to answer the door."

"Oh," Nanette said, as she felt a rush of color descend on her cheeks, "Caroline should be down shortly."

"No hurry, no hurry at all." The boy closed the door and stood in the foyer, flashing his killer smile at his date's little sister.

Nanette was aware that a full flirtation was coming at her. Although a bit taken aback by the attention, she did not mind it one bit. In fact, she was enjoying it—until Caroline came thumping down the steps, flashed a sharp look for Nanette's eyes only, and then turned her attention to her quarterback.

"So looking forward to seeing Cary Grant in …" Caroline lifted her finger as though trying to remember.

"*Charade*," the quarterback said, slanting a devilish smile at Nanette before returning his attention to Caroline.

Ah, sisterly rivalries, Nanette thought as she turned a corner on her bike. Up ahead, the Pleasantville town square came into view. She parked her bike at the edge of town at a bike rack in front of the post office, a one-story stone structure with arched windows and a cupola.

Nanette passed a boutique, its storefront window displaying mannequins in fashionable casual outfits. Next door was a bookstore with a tabby sleeping on the front window ledge. Nanette leaned against the window; inside were nooks and shelves packed with books that she imagined were old and dusty. Farther down, she stopped at a restaurant and read the daily specials on a chalkboard and then the menu in a glass case on a stand. Tables were set up under an awning, which brought to mind a bistro in Paris where she and Roger had dined during the trip to celebrate their twenty-fifth anniversary.

Nanette had enjoyed everything about Paris—strolling along the Champs-Élysées, Notre Dame, the museums, the restaurant, and two vineyard tours. For once, Roger had been a trouper, though by the end, he was worn out from all the walking, rich food, and wine.

More than drinking wine, which Roger enjoyed—red wine, in particular—he read, with great interest, books and articles on the history of wine and the process of making it. When they purchased *his* dream home, a refurbished Victorian in Chevy Chase, Roger had a temperature-controlled room built to store his wine. Wine and real estate had consumed much of Roger's time; his wife and son were afterthoughts.

Connor had been a forward on his high school soccer team, and Nanette showed for every game, home and away. Roger never made a game until the county championship in Connor's senior year, but he left at halftime, telling Nanette, "I need to get back to the office—big closings today."

Nanette knew it was no use trying to persuade her husband to stay, but after the game, during which Connor had won with the winning shot, his triumphant face dropped when he was met outside the locker room by only his mother. "Let me guess," he said with a concurring nod to Nanette. "Work."

It was as though once Roger had won Nanette over, married her, and had a son, it was time to move on to the next challenge—making money. And once he had established a successful real estate company with a competent staff, he moved on to wine.

Nanette took one last look at the restaurant, thinking how nice it might be to enjoy a meal and a glass of wine on the patio under the awning. Could she possibly go by herself? Never in her life had she ever dined alone; it was always with Roger and other couples or lunch with women. Going solo was something to consider in her new paradigm.

Still farther down, Nanette came upon the local theater, which she had missed on her first pass through town. The exterior looked to have been jury-rigged with a white wooden marquee attached to the front—PLEASANTVILLE THEATER COMPANY was in black block letters—a Plexiglas box office anchored by a wooden base, and glass panels on the exterior walls that listed the dates and times for auditions for *The Glass Menagerie.*

Nanette had not acted since college, only doing imitations of famous scenes from movies at parties in their old neighborhood in Bethesda, always to Roger's embarrassment. This would happen after a glass of wine or two, when Nanette was among friends who would encourage, "Do Stel-la-a-a."

Nanette would demur, though not so strongly as to not encourage her requester. "Come on, Nanette," he would beg. "I live for your performances."

A small gathering of people would wander over, and Nanette would gather herself, clear her throat, and let out a dead-on impression of Marlon Brando's version.

She also did a spot-on Jack Nicholson in *The Last Detail,* when he told a bartender in no uncertain terms that he was the motherfucking shore patrol. Nanette had loved that movie—the freedom, the time period, the way Nicholson swaggered about; it was a marvelous performance. She would never have thought to say such coarse language in general conversation, but a glass of wine and her acting instincts would win the day. And to his credit, though not pleased by these *antics*, as he called them, Roger never insisted she stop.

But once they moved to their more exclusive neighborhood in Chevy Chase, the mock performances ended. The move had been all Roger. Nanette had been happy and comfortable in their Ayrlawn community of middle-class to refurbished upper-middle-class homes, where they had moved in 1975, the year Connor was born, and left the year after Connor finished high school. Nanette had a core group of good friends, women like her who graduated from college and went into the workforce, married, had children, and might or might not have continued at their jobs while raising a family.

Nanette, who graduated as a married woman with a degree in liberal arts, got a job working in the administration office of a hotel chain. Her title was administration associate, which included reviewing documents for grammatical errors, typing out contracts, filing, and other paper-pushing chores. But after three years, Connor was born, and Nanette took a three-month leave of absence before she and Roger decided she should become a stay-at-home mom; her dreams of acting faded away like a thief in the night.

After obtaining his MBA, Roger went to work for a real estate investment trust and fast-tracked his way up the ladder. But he left the firm after seven years to develop Brinson Realty, a bold move with a stay-at-home wife and five-year-old son.

He was a good provider; I'll give him that, Nanette thought as she headed back toward her bike and the rest of her life.

CHAPTER 4

D EVIN DID AN ONLINE REAL estate search and discovered that Nanette Brinson was the purchaser of the bungalow. He googled her name and came up with an obituary for a Roger Brinson of Chevy Chase, Maryland, who had died the previous year and was survived by his wife, Nanette, and a son, who lived in New Zealand.

Devin had never known a Nanette, an old-fashioned name, though after returning home from Vietnam in 1971, he attended the Broadway show *No, No, Nanette,* a musical comedy that was a wonderful, farcical respite from a long and dangerous year building bridges and roads in the Mekong Delta. One thing that stuck out from the play all those years ago was the charming song "Tea for Two." He looked up the song and found that it was about dreaming of a romance with someone just met.

Devin knew it was crazy to leapfrog into fantasizing about a woman he had yet to meet. Only once in his life had he dived headfirst into a relationship, and that had not turned out well. After returning from Vietnam and being discharged, former Army First Lieutenant Devin McCortland returned to his parents' home in Hartford, Connecticut, to figure out what was next. After a couple of weeks of R&R, he bought a 1959 Austin-Healey convertible and gave it a thorough tune-up—new valves and sparkplugs, cleaned the carburetor, changed oil and filter, and checked all the wires. When he finished, the engine purred so smoothly that he thought it ready for a cross-country road trip.

His first stop was New York City, where he stayed at a college friend's apartment, hit the bars for a couple of nights, and saw *No, No, Nanette* after the friend's neighbor found out Devin had recently returned from Vietnam and gave them two tickets.

The neighbor was retired from a career as a stage manager in the theater. "I think a lighthearted comedy might be," the elderly man said, with index finger raised, "just what the doctor ordered." He offered a pronounced nod, as though the matter was settled.

And it was good medicine, as Devin sang songs from the play all the way down to Key West, where he slept on the beach and caroused at Ernest Hemingway's old haunt, Sloppy Joe's Bar. He then headed up the Gulf Coast and straight through to Texas in a little over twenty hours, which included a state trooper in Mississippi pulling him over for speeding.

After asking for his license and registration, the officer, a tall, big-shouldered man, studied Devin. "You military, son?" he asked in a deep baritone with an echo of the Old South.

"Yes, sir," Devin said, just as polite as could be. "I just returned from a tour in Vietnam."

The trooper nodded and handed Devin back his license and registration. "Where you headed?"

"West Coast."

"Slow down 'til you get to Texas. You are free to go."

It was drive and pull over, get gas and food, and catnap for a couple of hours until he made it to Manhattan Beach, California, a cozy little beach town where he had spent time before deploying to Vietnam.

While overseas, often before falling asleep, Devin would imagine lying on a blanket under the benevolent SoCal sun, with the sound of tall, floating waves pounding the beach; then bellying up to the Windsurfer's Bar or playing volleyball. Of course, the beautiful girls were everywhere in this windswept beach town.

Upon arriving, Devin got a motel room and slept for twenty-four, then rented a twelve-by-twelve space annexed from a two-story cottage right on the ocean. The room had a bathroom with a shower and a bunk bed—that was it and all he needed.

Soon, he got in a rhythm—morning jog, followed by a swim in the ocean, volleyball in the afternoon, and the Windsurfer or another bar in the evening. Along the way, Devin had a few one-night stands, one with a German flight attendant doing a layover from LAX, and another with a model in town doing a shoot on the beach. He never saw either one again.

But after a couple of weeks of this casual, go-with-the-flow life, Devin met a young woman, who had recently dropped out of college, at a volleyball tournament he was playing in. During the match, they had made eye contact, a flirting smile from her that he returned, a look-over after a winning point, and another round of *hello-there* looks.

Her name was Gretchen Winter, and she had a free-spiritedness that, after his year in Nam, was so very appealing to him. And to go with it, she was a bombshell, with long, thick chestnut hair that she wore in braids or a ponytail. Her face was wild and lovely with an insouciant look that emanated from deep brown eyes that seemed to hide some great mystery—or so it seemed at the time. And her body had curves in all the right places and long, strong legs.

Soon, they were an item, and Devin fell in love for the first time in his life. There had been previous girlfriends, but this was his first true-blue romance. Three weeks in, Devin thought he had found the woman to spend the rest of his life with. But Gretchen had other ideas. She told Devin that she was heading back home to Omaha—"To finish school and get myself straight." She offered a hand in farewell—"It's been real."

Devastated, Devin went on a drinking binge for three days and nights before he'd had enough. Two weeks later, he headed back home, taking his time, and eventually found employment working for a major construction company, traveling around the country, working mostly on highway construction. He retired after thirty-five years and decided on Pleasantville, where he had stayed a few years back while working on a bridge repair on Interstate 75.

Looking back, he realized that he had been vulnerable after the war—the things he had seen, the lives lost, the waste of it all. With her carefree hippie way, Gretchen had reeled him right in, and he went for her hook, line, and sinker. Not that he regretted it, but if they had married, would they have stayed together? They didn't really know each other—two young people at a crossroads.

But now, with Nanette Brinson, it all seemed different. They were no longer kids but adults, mature adults—she, a widow; he, a man in search of—what, he was not sure. But he would soon see where it led. Tomorrow, he would knock on her door.

CHAPTER 5

NANETTE SAT ON THE BACK patio, tired but satisfied. After three days in her new home, she had things pretty well organized. Family photos, clothes and shoes, and a few other personal items—all of which she had packaged and mailed to the Pleasantville Post Office—had arrived yesterday. She arranged clothes and shoes in her spacious walk-in closet. Framed photos of various phases of Connor's childhood were placed around the house; she put one on her dresser of her and Roger at a wine tasting in Paris. It was such an unusual photo—Roger, beaming, his arm around Nanette's shoulder; a quizzical grin slashed her face as if to say, *Is this really happening?*

Roger was different from any of the boys Nanette had previously dated. Stout and intense, with a thrash of dark curly hair, her first sight of him was on a scaffold as he worked on the overhead stage lights during a dress rehearsal for *Streetcar Named Desire*.

The director, a graduate student working on his doctorate in theater, hollered at Roger, "Hey, light man."

Roger slanted a look down. "Yeah," he replied in a challenging voice.

"How about holding up until we finish here."

"How about," Roger said, "you do your thing, and I'll do mine." He waited a moment, as though for effect, and turned back around, but his attention was diverted by Nanette, wearing a strapless organdy dress that the director had insisted she wear. She thought it a bit risqué with its plunging neckline, straining her bodice that fit like a glove. He threw her a wink and went back to his lights.

Nanette had previously dated boys who were athletes or members of the in-crowd. There had been two semi-serious relationships, one boy in high school and one in college, and more casual dating in between. Nanette was a virgin before Roger and only came close once, during her senior year in high school at a drive-in movie, when she had too much to drink. Right before the deed was done, she hollered an emphatic *no*, and the boy relented.

Roger had the confidence of someone older, never pushing himself on Nanette, though slowly and surely casting his spell on her. He was more mature and serious, with a game plan for life after school. "By thirty, I want to own my own company," he told Nanette on their first date at a family-run Italian restaurant. "Not sure what type of company, but I want to call my own shots."

Thanksgiving break of her senior year, Nanette and Roger said *I do* at a small ceremony for family and a few close friends. Nanette had always dreamed of a big wedding, but Roger nixed it. "Waste of our parents' money." And Nanette's father, who had recently paid handsomely for Caroline's wedding, agreed. "Level-headed young man," he would say more than once.

Before Roger came along, Nanette had dreamed that after college, she would head to New York or Hollywood and find a menial job while taking acting classes and trying to break into the business of performing. It was a scary proposition, leaving home, finding a place to live and a roommate, and being a young woman out on her own, trying to make her way.

She liked to tell herself that if she hadn't met Roger, whom she felt confident would provide for her and take care of her, she would have taken the leap—she'd have told Mom and Dad that she was heading to Los Angeles, which she thought more glamorous and safer than New York. But would she have done it? *Water under the bridge*, she thought as she eyed the raised garden bed swarming with weeds. She'd had a garden in her Bethesda and Chevy Chase houses, but one raised bed was not enough. She wanted tomatoes in one and root vegetables in the other.

She entered the kitchen and got the handyman's card from a drawer. She had never heard of a *McCortland*—Scottish? Devin McCortland had a good ring to it—*the Scottish ambassador Devin McCortland* or a highlander tribal leader dressed in a kilt, ghillie shirt, and sporran.

Nanette was startled by a knock at the front door.

At the front window, she saw a pickup truck parked in the driveway, with *McCortland Handyman Service* scrolled on the driver's side door.

She opened the door.

"Hello, Devin McCortland, here. I believe Ed Feldman gave you my card."

"Oh," Nanette said, as she discovered she was still holding his business card. "I was just about to call you."

In a momentary pause, she took in the man before her: around six foot two, broad shoulders, strong-looking and fit, with a boyishly handsome countenance on a mature face. He brought to mind a young old boy, wearing khaki shorts, gray T-shirt, and low-cut sneakers—he looked athletic. Also in that moment, something like an understanding passed—a *mutual like*. She intuited that he was single; why that was, she wasn't sure. Maybe it was the way he looked at her with a flicker of interest—an I'd-like-to-get-to-know-you look.

"Must be karma," Devin said through an easy smile. "What can I help you with?"

Nanette led Devin through the house to the back patio. "I would like another raised garden bed like the one you built."

Devin stood next to Nanette, studying the yard, which was approximately twenty-five by twenty-five feet; the shed in the back corner; and the raised garden bed along the back fence. "Maybe three feet over," he said, glancing at Nanette.

"Just what I was thinking." Nanette smiled her golden-girl smile at this hunky handyman.

Devin went over the type of material for the job and the cost, which Nanette accepted.

"I can write up a contract if you like," Devin said with a shrug.

"Not necessary. When could you start?"

Devin squinted as though pondering. "I'm tied up for the rest of the week. How about next Monday morning at eight?"

CHAPTER 6

IT HAD BEEN A GOOD long while since a woman had stirred Devin, an aroused stir. The rest of the workweek and through the weekend, his mind drifted to Nanette Brinson. It seemed strange that at sixty-four, this circumstance was occurring. His entire being was riveted by a sense of anticipation of going to a woman's home and building a raised garden bed.

He tried to slow it down, but it was no use. Sunday evening, he sipped on a beer on his back deck, which he had built right after he purchased his ranch-style, three-bedroom, no-frills house. He would begin building the raised garden the following day. He had all the material loaded in the pickup parked underneath the carport. This would normally be a two-day job, but Devin pondered how to stretch it out. He wasn't sure how much she would be around when he was working, though he thought it a strong possibility that she'd be there. She had been friendly toward him—not overly so, but he thought he had seen a glimmer of interest in her gaze the first time they made eye contact. There had been a momentary pause as a look of approval came over her face, a look that said, *Well, hello there.*

Devin was never sure about interpreting a look from a woman. Was it his imagination? He was out of practice with the opposite sex. He had lived in Pleasantville for four years since his retirement, and over that time, he had been out with two different women, and each date had ended poorly. The first was right after he moved to Pleasantville with a woman he had met at a nearby park; he'd helped her find her lost dog.

They met for a beer at a local pub and ended up back at Devin's place for a night of uninhibited sex. But the following morning, she confessed to being married. "But my husband travels for business, and we could see each other when he's away."

Devin told her no.

She went on to say that her husband was twenty years older than she and had little interest in sex. "I'm his trophy wife. He likes to show me off to his friends and business colleagues," she said, as a look of desperation flashed over her face.

Devin was tempted, for she was a fortysomething blonde bombshell who possessed everything that a man could desire in regard to physical attraction, but there was an air of artificiality hovering over her, and combined with her being married, he stayed firm.

Devin met the second woman at the grocery store. She asked Devin if he could reach up on the top shelf for a box of detergent. They got to talking, and the next thing Devin knew, he was in a serious relationship. Her name was Rose. She had married young, had a daughter, and divorced a louse of a husband. After working thirty years as a claims adjuster, she had retired to Pleasantville.

On their first date, Rose spilled that she had lived in Pleasantville for two months and lately had been crying herself to sleep at night from loneliness. "It's not as easy for a fifty-year-old woman to make a new life for herself as it is for a man."

They dated for a month before Rose decided to move back home to Pennsylvania. "My daughter is having a baby and has asked me to live with her and her family."

Part of Devin was sad to see her go—she was an uncomplicated woman who liked pleasing Devin, be it in bed or in cooking succulent meals—but there was a clinginess to her that could get wearisome.

So for the last eighteen months, Devin had not been with a woman—nary a date—and he hadn't paid it much mind until he laid eyes on Nanette Brinson, and everything changed.

Well, sir, he thought as he finished his beer, *stay tuned, for tomorrow can't come soon enough.*

CHAPTER 7

O N MONDAY MORNING, NANETTE WOKE at dawn and slipped into
shorts, a T-shirt, and a pair of Nike running shoes. She took a walk
around the neighborhood, wandering in and out of different sections
of her community, looking around, and taking it in. The homes were
all similar sizes—ramblers and bungalows, mostly. As she was about
to turn around and head back home, she spotted Devin's truck in the
carport of a rambler. This early, it must be his home, or could it be a
lady friend's place?

But there was only his truck; no other cars were around. If he had a
wife, there would be another vehicle, and if he had a girlfriend, Nanette
figured her car would be there, especially since Devin was scheduled
to begin work on the raised bed at eight, less than an hour from now.

As Nanette headed back home, an idea sprang on her. It was a bold
thought: ask Devin to join her for lunch on the patio. Could she do it?
It was like asking him out, almost. She decided she would play it by ear.

After a shower, Nanette put on a pair of clamdiggers—Roger had
told her that they revealed just enough of her legs to want to see
more—a short-sleeved pleated blouse, and sandals. At the bathroom
mirror, she ran a brush through her wavy honey-gold hair that had lost
none of its youthful luster, though flecks of gray were emerging on the
sides. Nanette had thought about a dye job but had resisted. She decided
to tie the back in a ponytail that hung above her shoulders.

She studied her face. A line creased out on both corners of her blue-
green eyes, but the face was devoid of any major flaws, the chin still
firm. Nanette knew she was fortunate to look this way at her age. A
couple of years ago at her fortieth high school reunion, she was shocked
by how many of her classmates had aged, especially the women; if not

for name tags on their chests, she would have never guessed who some of them were. Roger had not gone, telling Nanette he would just hold her back. She had been glad that he decided against going, as her main squeeze in high school, Jimmy Manion—the boy she almost went too far with at the drive-in—showed up.

Jimmy looked more handsome than ever. He had been number one on the tennis team and one of the most popular boys in the class. Of average size, his body still maintained a lean and sinewy design, his face maintained a chiseled handsomeness, and his once jet-black hair had turned salt-and-pepper that gave him a distinguished look. Nanette knew Jimmy would probably head to the bar, so she made a beeline for it and stood in line.

"Nanette Brinson, you look fabulous," an approaching Jimmy said through a gorgeous smile, his teeth like deep-water gems.

Nanette had not seen Jimmy Manion since he went off to college on the West Coast and stayed there. They took a seat in a corner and caught up. Jimmy, who said he was divorced with two grown children, now went by James and had been successful in the hotel/motel business. He had sold out of it and now was investing in Hollywood films. He asked if she had continued to act. "You were so good as Lady Macbeth, senior year."

"No," Nanette replied, "I didn't." She heard the disappointment in her voice.

"Well, if you ever get the urge," James said, "give me a call." He handed her his card. "Your talent should be on display."

But it wasn't until Roger's passing and after the shock had subsided that she decided on her life alterations. Of course so far, she had moved to Florida, but she had yet to sign up for the audition at the local theater that was to begin in a couple of weeks.

As she turned from the mirror, she decided to consider the audition a bit more while she concentrated on her raised bed and the fellow who was coming to construct it.

CHAPTER 8

DEVIN LOOSENED THE BUNGEE CORDS and pulled his contractor's wheelbarrow out of the bed of his pickup that he had parked in Nanette's driveway; upon arrival, he had discovered her car parked on the street. He then unloaded a pair of sawhorses, a four-foot level, a mattock, a flat shovel, a tamper, a tool bucket, and stakes into the wheelbarrow and pushed it into Nanette's backyard.

After four more trips of hauling the cedar boards, plastic hoops, mesh covering, and some miscellaneous pieces, Devin was ready to begin. He took some measurements, hammered his stakes for the bed's exterior, ran a string line connecting the stakes, and began digging up the grass with his mattock.

After he had dug out the grass, he told himself to slow it down, but it was against Devin's nature to do such a thing—work slow, no; but sit, yes. So he took a break and had a seat at a wrought-iron table on the flagstone patio that he had built.

The weather was warm but comfortable, though with a chance of afternoon showers. Devin always checked the weather first thing every morning. It was essential when he was doing masonry jobs, not wanting the rain to destroy the drying mortar. On this job, it would be more of a nuisance than a problem, but it could stretch out the job.

Devin heard the sliding door to the patio open.

"I see you don't waste any time," Nanette said as she approached, eyeing the bare rectangle patch.

"Oh," Devin said, looking up with a shrug, "nice soft ground makes for fast work." He wanted to ask Nanette to have a seat but thought it forward since it was her house. "Thanks for parking your car on the street."

Nanette smiled, as if to say, *No big deal.* She seemed to start to speak but hesitated. She smiled a shy smile, her mouth crimped in the corners, her eyes squinting. "I made a ton of shrimp salad and wondered if you might want to join me for lunch."

"That'd be great," Devin said. "What time were you thinking?"

"I have some errands to run—say, twelve?"

"Shall we eat here?" Devin said, offering his hand to the table.

"Shrimp salad and ice tea al fresco, it is," Nanette said. She tapped her knuckles on the metal mesh tabletop, followed by a radiant smile that seemed to register an inner kindness of spirit.

After Nanette left, Devin began leveling the ground with his flat shovel and then checked with the four-foot level. After the patch was level, he began cutting the lumber and assembling, always double-checking as he went along.

After years of working on large construction jobs with big crews, Devin enjoyed the solitude and quiet of working on his own—no one else for whom he was responsible, no problems with personalities not getting along, just Devin McCortland and his tools.

In some ways, it was rather mundane work for someone with his skill set, but it kept him busy and not harping on his failed life: never married; no children; most of his existence a peripatetic adventure of staying in a place from six months to two years and then moving on; living in apartments or rented homes, at first with a roommate or two but later going solo.

In between assignments, he would return to his parents' home in Hartford before buying his own place, more as an investment. "Buying a home, even if you're not there that often, is a good, solid investment," his father told him, and Devin agreed. Having paid the house off years ago, he made a nice profit when he sold it after deciding to move to Pleasantville.

He had worked his way up the ladder to engineering superintendent, a stressful, challenging job in which he had to meet deadlines and work in inhospitable weather, and he had the daily grind of arising at five o'clock in the morning. But Vietnam had been an excellent, though brutal, training ground for his career.

First Lieutenant McCortland and his team often worked twelve-hour days, building bridges in hot, humid weather; during the rainy season, they were constantly under attack from swarms of mosquitoes the size of cockroaches, as well as vigilantly being on the lookout for Vietcong snipers. Devin lost only one man from his team of fifteen, and it was not from enemy fire but malaria; two others were wounded in firefights, but they not only recovered but got sent home early.

Devin lost thirty-five pounds in that God-awful war, and even more, he lost faith in his government. He thought the war a complete waste, from the lives lost to the money spent to the division it caused back home.

Over the last few years, a thought had crept into Devin's head that Vietnam had a much greater effect on the direction of his life than he had ever imagined. After graduating from college with a degree in civil engineering, and instead of waiting to get drafted, he enlisted in OCS, but had to do two months of basic training at Fort Polk, Louisiana, followed by twenty-three grueling weeks of OCS at Fort Belvoir, Virginia, and ten weeks attending engineer training at Fort Leonard Wood in the Ozarks and then, finally, off to Nam.

After Vietnam, he received an early discharge that he thought was partly due to his weakened physical condition, as though Devin was no longer of use.

The whole affair of military service had left a mark on Devin, a profound sense that asked, *What's it all about?* Soon after his cross-country road trip to Manhattan Beach and the heartbreaking affair with the beguiling and beautiful Gretchen Winter, Devin signed on to work on repairing a bridge in Harrisburg, Pennsylvania. Talk about a change of scenery.

He looked back on his working with different people in all those different jobs in all those different locales. He'd had a relationship with a woman in nearly every town without committing to any. He realized now that he was damaged goods. He had been a man on the run.

Devin's last job for the firm was a highway not far from Pleasantville, where he rented a house for nine months. The place had a quieting effect; the pace was slow, and the weather was too warm in the summer, but at the end of the job, he handed in his resignation and decided to stay—never looking back. But now, what was there to look forward to—easy-as-you-go small jobs, beers at a local tavern on weekends or a quick beer or two during the week, talking sports with some of the regulars but never letting anyone too close?

Devin had a few casual friends he had met through his work. He attended neighborhood barbeques and played tennis from time to time with Ed Feldman and some of his friends, but there was a wall, an impenetrable wall that Devin had subconsciously constructed to keep people from getting inside.

But for some reason, he thought he would allow Nanette Brinson entry.

CHAPTER 9

NANETTE SAT AT THE OAK table in her home office, staring at her laptop screen. She had filled out the audition form, and now all she had to do was click *send*. A waver of fear stirred in her stomach. She hadn't acted in nearly forty years. Did she still possess the talent? Maybe she should wait until she was more settled in Pleasantville.

A car door closing drew her attention to the front window. Devin had a power drill in one hand and a box of screws in the other and was briskly walking toward the backyard. She knew little about him, only assumptions. Hopefully, at lunch, she would learn more. She was pretty sure that he wasn't married by the glint in his eyes when he accepted her lunch invitation. It was a look of interest, a look that said, *That sounds mighty fine.*

She had considered a people search but thought it prying, though she did wonder if he had done a search on her. And if so, did he know she was a recent widow, nearly sixty years old at that?

Nanette returned her attention to the computer screen and the audition form. If she was going to start a new life, she had to get outside her comfort zone. She pressed her index finger on the mouse and scrolled up to *send*. She held it there for a moment—the moment of truth. "Go big or go home," she said aloud. She pressed her finger down, and her reply was off into the ether.

A message appeared on the screen: *Thank you for your submission. We will get back with you on the time of your audition.*

What would Roger think of his wife moving on less than six months after his passing? If it had been the other way around, he might well have fallen for a woman who had a similar interest in wine—such as the fortysomething owner of a vineyard in Charlottesville, Virginia, who had offered samples of a cabernet and a Chablis at a winetasting at a hotel in DC. Roger hit it right off with this female vintner.

Soon, they were discussing aeration and fermentation and sinking deeper into winemaking lingo, as if they were members of a secret club. Roger grew animated, his eyes wide with interest in not only the topic but the woman before him. Nanette stood there like an afterthought.

After tasting the wines, Roger offered a nod of approval. "The red is full-bodied and has an excellent bouquet; the white is light yet pleasing." Roger bought two bottles each and asked if she shipped.

"Yes," the vintner responded with a smile, "but only by the case."

Roger returned her smile with his own ear-to-ear grin. "Like I always say, go big or go home."

A few weeks later, Roger told Nanette that he was going to Charlottesville to tour a couple of vineyards. "You're welcome to come," he told her in a flat tone, "but it is going to be all about wine."

"Where are you staying?" Nanette inquired as she felt her throat tighten.

"Joy has a cottage on her property that she said I was welcome to use."

"Joy?"

"The vintner from the winetasting," Roger replied in an even, no-big-deal tone.

Oh, but it was a big deal; it was the moment Nanette realized her marriage had entered new territory.

CHAPTER 10

B Y NOON, DEVIN HAD THE six-foot-by-three-foot planter assembled and set in the ground. He had lost himself in the process and worked faster than he wanted, but he still had to pick up bags of topsoil and compost to fill the planter and then erect the hoops and mesh covering.

As he flicked sawdust off his arms and shirt, he saw Nanette come outside, holding a basket of napkins and utensils.

She placed the basket on the table and said, "I'll be right back."

"Can I help?" Devin asked.

"Yes," Nanette said, "if you could get the tray of drinks on the kitchen counter, I will get the rest.

Devin followed her inside. "Wow," he said as he eyed a bowl of shrimp salad, as well as sourdough bread, sliced green tomatoes, diced lettuce, and condiments on a tray. "This sure beats peanut butter and jelly on rye."

Nanette laughed. "I hope I'm not spoiling you." She lifted the tray, smiled at Devin, and headed for the door.

After Devin had dressed his sandwich, he took a hearty bite. "Oh, that is delicious," he said earnestly.

"It's an old family recipe," Nanette said, as she spooned shrimp salad onto her plate.

Devin felt comfortable sitting on Nanette's patio, sharing a meal. She had a soothing aura about her—a vibe of joyful tranquility. He decided to make a confession. "I looked you up online." He searched her face for a reaction.

Nanette laughed heartily. "I was going to do the same thing for you but chickened out."

"Ah," Devin said, "not sure you would have found much very interesting. Sorry about your husband."

"Thank you," Nanette said. She sunk her fork into her shrimp salad and held it for a moment before taking a bite.

Devin felt a bit awkward, doing this social dance, and decided to take a chance. "The real reason I knocked on your door was because I wanted to meet you."

Nanette made a face, a question in her eyes.

"As chance would have it," Devin said, "I drove by your house the day you moved in."

"And?" Nanette said in a tone that encouraged him to continue.

"I said to myself"—Devin took a *here-goes* breath—"I need to meet that woman."

"And now," Nanette said as her eyes brightened, "here we are."

After some small talk about Nanette's new house and the weather, Nanette asked Devin how long he had lived in Pleasantville. That led to Devin giving a quick review of his life: growing up in Connecticut, college, building bridges in Vietnam, cross-country trip to Manhattan Beach (he didn't mention Gretchen), and his career. "And no kids and never been married."

Nanette told him about growing up in Bethesda, Maryland—"It was the happiest time of my life"—her participation in theater, and getting married while still an undergraduate. "Other than having my son, my marriage was the biggest mistake of my life." She arched an eyebrow pensively, her lovely eyes taking in Devin, as though to gauge his interest. "My marriage was pretty much a formality by the time my husband passed."

"Funny," Devin said as he lifted his sandwich, "I always thought the biggest mistake of my life was never getting married and having children." He took a chomp, swelling his cheek. "Of course, the one woman I would have married most likely would have been a disaster."

"Oh?" Nanette said in an inquisitive tone.

"I was still damaged goods from Vietnam, and I fell hard—too hard, in Manhattan Beach, no less." He exhaled through his teeth as the memory flashed in his mind. "It was not meant to be."

"As painful as it was," Nanette said in a soft, understanding voice, "it might have been a blessing, considering where you were at that stage of your life."

After they finished eating, Devin helped Nanette clear the table. Inside the kitchen, he placed the plates and silverware on the counter next to the sink. "Well, I better get back at it. I appreciate the lunch and the conversation."

Nanette stopped rinsing the plates with the sink sprayer. "I enjoyed your company," she said with a smirk, as though hoping for something more.

"Would you like to go out for a drink and maybe dinner sometime?" Devin made a face. *What do you think?*

"Yes," Nanette said, "I would like that."

"Friday good?"

"Yes," Nanette said as her heart-melting eyes looked at Devin. "Friday, it is."

CHAPTER 11

AFTER LUNCH, NANETTE SET UP her laptop at the kitchen nook, where she had a view of Devin working in the backyard. She googled "*The Glass Menagerie*" and read a synopsis of the play. It was the story of a faded Southern belle, Amanda Wingfield, and her grown children, Tom and Laura, all living under the same roof. As with all Tennessee Williams plays, there was much strife and conflict.

She lifted her gaze over her reading glasses and watched Devin cutting mesh with wire snips. He was a fine figure of a man who moved with an easy confidence, as though he were handling a task in his wheelhouse.

She had gathered from talking with him that he had not lived the happiest of lives—a lonely existence, traveling from town to town, building a road or repairing a bridge, never establishing roots. She found him so different from Roger, not only in appearance but in personality.

Devin had an affable way about him, even though there was a *what-if* in his demeanor, as if he regretted the life he had lived. It was exciting, though a bit unsettling, to be going out on a date with a man she had just met, a man who admitted he had knocked on her door because he had wanted to meet her after a quick drive-by.

After all these years, Nanette had no idea that she could still have such an effect on a man. Would he play it slow and not try to kiss her at some point during their first time together? She assumed there would be a second time. And at some point, would they have sex?

Her first time with Roger had taken place on their fourth date, after Nanette had three glasses of wine to fortify herself for the loss of her virginity. It wasn't nearly as painful as she had thought it would be, and the wine allowed her to enjoy the physical thrusting and intimacy of a man entering her.

But after Connor was born, Roger, who always initiated sex, lost interest—at least in sex with his wife. Once or twice a month was all that he volunteered for. Nanette wasn't sure what to make of it. She didn't think there was another woman but that Roger, absorbed in his career, seemed to have little time for anything else, including his wife and son, to whom he paid only perfunctory attention.

Later on in the marriage, after he sold his business and got interested in wine, Nanette thought that he more than likely engaged in extramarital affairs, especially with the female vintner in Charlottesville.

Nanette had not had sex in years—she wasn't even sure how many. The thought of lying naked with Devin sent a tingle down her spine that settled in her loins. Having only been with one man in her life and that having been so long ago, it might well be a very pleasurable experience to make love to that hunky, interesting fellow building her raised bed, though the thought of another man seeing her naked gave her pause—the old yin-yang dilemma.

She returned to her laptop, downloaded a copy of the play, and began to read. There were only four major roles, and Nanette was suited for only one—Amanda, who was abandoned by her husband, which Nanette could relate to. Though she didn't live in the harsh economic circumstances that Amanda had, Nanette could sink herself into the emotional state of a woman who had been deserted by her man, if not in physical distance but emotionally.

A tapping turned Nanette's attention to the back door. She got up and opened the sliding glass door.

"May I use your bathroom?" Devin asked.

"Down the foyer on the right."

Nanette returned to the table and her laptop and waited.

When Devin returned, he waved a thank-you, as though not wanting to disturb.

"Do you need water or anything to drink?"

"I'm good," Devin replied. He motioned toward the laptop computer. "I got one last year. It's great for communicating with clients and storing invoices and the like."

"How did we ever get by without one?" Nanette said. She threw her hand toward the screen. "I'm looking over a play I just downloaded—amazing."

"A play, you say," Devin said in a tone that said, *Tell me more.*

"I used to act in theater in college, and I'm going to audition for a part in *The Glass Menagerie* by Tennessee Williams at the local theater."

"Amanda Wingfield?" Devin asked, as if he already knew the answer.

"How did you know, and how do you know Amanda Wingfield?"

"Lincoln, Nebraska, a few years back," Devin said, "I was on a job, and the wife of one of the contractors I became friends with played the part in a local theater. She was really good, as was the play."

Nanette let out a little *huh*. "That's amazing."

"I bet you are a good actress," Devin said with an affirming nod.

"I like to think I was." Nanette glanced at the computer screen and then back at Devin. "But it's been almost forty years."

"I bet it's like riding a bike," Devin said as he reached for the door. "Once a good actress, always a good actress."

CHAPTER 12

EVIN BACKED HIS PICKUP OUT of Nanette's driveway and headed the short distance to his home. After a shower and changing into a fresh T-shirt, shorts, and flip-flops, he put some leftover vegetarian chili on the stovetop and made an arugula salad with peeled carrot, diced red peppers, red onion, and cherry tomatoes.

He got a bottle of Coors out of the fridge and took a seat on his back deck. The overcast sky had cleared without any rain, and a gentle breeze from the west carried the sweet scent of cypress trees. His yard was similar to Nanette's, with a couple of indigenous trees—cypress and Florida maple—a picket fence, and a shed in a back corner. There was not a lot of diversity in the layout of the properties or the size of the homes, mostly three bedrooms with two-and-a-half baths, patio or wood deck in back, and a neatly trimmed, smallish yard of predominantly Bermuda or Zoysia grass.

There also was a cookie-cutter quality to the neighborhood, but it had suited Devin at the time of purchase. There was a no-muss/no-fuss simplicity about the place, which, after years of traveling from town to town and working long hours on noisy, dusty projects, appealed to him at the time and mostly still did—though ennui had begun to set in as each day and week and month had a been-there/done-that quality.

But all that had changed. The paradigm of Devin's existence had taken a turn. Today had been a good day, not only the progress he had made on the raised bed but securing a date with Nanette, a woman who had awakened a stirring in him that he had thought extinguished. With everything she said, every smile, or when she settled her gaze on him and him alone, it was as though it was just the two of them in a heightened state to the promises of life.

Devin had not felt like this since falling in love as a young man with Gretchen in Manhattan Beach, which seemed more like someone else's life at this point. He wasn't in love—not yet—but he could see himself allowing it to happen. And he thought Nanette was in the same state of mind.

He could not imagine being married to such a woman and not paying attention to her. And what type of man showed little interest in a son?

Looking back, his not having a child was a huge regret. To have helped bring a young life into adulthood, to watch him or her fail and try again, to strive forward and take on life. He had watched the progressive maturation of his friends' children in the different towns he worked in—the pride on the faces of the fathers of newborns, the happy stories during the toddler years, and the worries of the teenage years. But through it all, Devin could see how the connection to your own flesh and blood forged an unbreakable link.

With no family—his parents dead and no siblings—Devin's closest link was cousins with whom he hadn't been in touch since he left for college. He took a swig of his beer; the cool, sudsy liquid washed down his throat. Drinking a beer and thinking things over was a necessary part of Devin's existence. He didn't drink every night—usually Wednesday, Friday, and sometimes Saturday were his libation breaks. But on this Monday night, he made an exception, as he needed to drink a few cold ones and contemplate Nanette Brinson.

Devin arrived at Nanette's house at a quarter to eight and waited in her driveway. Work couldn't begin in Pleasantville until eight, but he always arrived early on a job, an old habit from his engineering days when he double-checked the previous day's work.

"Good morning."

Startled, Devin turned to his open window, and there stood Nanette in low-cut sneakers, short shorts, and a T-shirt that hugged her curvy torso. She was achingly fine-looking.

"Morning run?"

Nanette shook her head. "Morning walk. I was never much for running."

"I used to run half-marathons when I was younger, but around fifty, my Achilles tendon told me that walking might be a better option."

"Walk, don't run," Nanette said as she flicked a strand of hair off her brow and beamed one of her beauteous smiles on Devin. They looked at each other for a moment before Nanette said, "Would you join me for an herbal tea before you begin work?"

"Yes," Devin said as he opened the door, "that would be great."

Nanette served the tea on the patio, sitting across from Devin. "I put honey in your tea." Nanette slanted an inquisitive look at Devin.

"Now, how did you know that was how I liked my tea?" he teased. Devin was aware that a flirt was on, and he was enjoying it immensely.

"You look like a honey kind of guy," Nanette said as she lifted her cup and took a careful sip, her eyes remaining on Devin.

"Well," Devin said as he lifted his cup and held it, "I am going to take that as a compliment." He took a swallow and placed his cup back on the table.

"So," Nanette said in a more serious tone, "when do you think you will finish?" She looked to her left at the unfinished raised bed.

"If I pushed it, I could finish today." Devin lifted his brow to Nanette, as if asking, *What do you think?*

"There's no hurry," Nanette said. "Why don't you finish up tomorrow?"

CHAPTER 13

NANETTE SAT AT THE KITCHEN nook, having finished reading *The Glass Menagerie*. She was not fond of Amanda Wingfield, a controlling, unlikeable woman who was past her prime. But she remembered that her job as an actress was not to like her character but to understand her and, through that understanding, project to the audience every flaw and idiosyncrasy that the writer intended to exploit.

She lifted her gaze to the backyard, where Devin was finishing up the raised bed. He was shoveling compost from his wheelbarrow into the planter. The mesh had been attached to the pliable hoops that folded back, allowing easy access. She had watched him work, his skill obvious, as he measured, cut, and beveled in assembling a beautiful cedar work of art.

As agreed, Devin had taken his time on the job, today being Wednesday. Yesterday and today, they'd had lunch on the patio, and each time Nanette had grown more comfortable and at ease with this talented man, but at the same time, there was a certain mysteriousness to him. How could such a good-looking, appealing man have lived such a life of traveling about the country from city to city, with no family to go home to and no one to love? Was there something in his past—Vietnam or the unrequited love in Manhattan Beach, which he had offhandedly commented on—that had sent him off-kilter on his life journey?

Whatever it was, it had brought him to her at this point in time, in this town called Pleasantville in Central Florida, where second and third acts in life were possible. And maybe he was looking at her in the same light—an attractive woman who had stayed married to an unloving husband, whose death had ultimately allowed her freedom. Nanette told herself not to overthink but to go with the flow.

By midafternoon, Devin was putting away his tools, with the job complete. Nanette thought it perfect— two raised garden beds in the rear of her yard, three feet apart. They added a craftsman's touch, along with her attractive shed with its gently sloping roof of cedar shingles, arched door, and window boxes with impatiens she had planted the other day.

As Devin approached the back door, Nanette got up and greeted him. "Beautiful job, Devin." She handed him a check. "Payment in full, Mr. Handyman."

"Thank you," he said as he folded the check and slipped it into the back pocket of his shorts. "Well ..." he said in a hesitant tone. "I will see you Friday."

Nanette didn't want to wait for over forty-eight hours to see this breath of fresh air that had suddenly entered her life. She scrunched up her face into a squinty, what-do-you-think smile. "Would you like to have dinner here tonight?"

Devin's eyes lit up, as though a switch had been turned on. "Yes," he said. "I would like that."

Nanette had much to do, for she hadn't planned for dinner, other than some leftovers. She went to the store, bought two salmon steaks, fresh-cut broccoli, sweet potatoes, and salad fixings.

Back home, she made a kale salad with diced apples, cranberries, and pecans. She then peeled and diced the sweet potatoes, sprinkled them with olive oil and seasoning, and stored them in the fridge. There was a gas grill on the back patio, and she hoped when she attempted to start it, Devin would volunteer to take over cooking the salmon.

She checked the clock hanging on the wall of the kitchen nook; she had an hour before Devin would arrive.

After a shower, she went into her closet to pick out what to wear for the night. She guessed that Devin would come in a polo shirt and shorts, and she decided on a casual outfit. She had always been a conservative dresser, never wearing miniskirts or low-cut dresses or blouses to display her cleavage. The first time Roger had felt her up, he later commented how surprised he was. "You really hide those generous ta-tas."

She picked out a white sleeveless blouse and Bermuda shorts—not too conservative and not too risqué.

After dressing, Nanette ran a brush through her hair at the bathroom mirror, studying her face. She could use a touch of mascara but decided against it. Devin seemed like the type who liked little makeup or perfume. She hadn't acted like this since college—primping to please a man.

Back in the kitchen, she set two places at the kitchen nook—the dining room was a drab, dead space. The nook had two tall windows that brought in welcoming sunlight and easy access to the kitchen and patio, where she placed a corkscrew and two wine glasses on the wrought-iron table. Devin had volunteered to bring wine—"We can have an aperitif on the patio and admire your new raised bed," he had said.

She returned to the kitchen and prepared a platter of rye crackers and a block of pepper jack cheese that she sliced. It wouldn't have been her first choice, but she thought it suited Devin's taste. She checked the time; she had fifteen minutes until Devin's arrival.

She took the platter out to the patio, pulled back a chair, and sat. She had been in Florida a little over a week, and here she was, waiting for a gentleman caller, and a fine-looking one at that. Other than Roger, Nanette had always been attracted to good-looking men—not that Roger was unattractive, but he wasn't the tall, dashing type; he was more the stout, manly man who oozed confidence and possessed an aggressive intelligence to back up his attitude. She had never met anyone like Roger, who had stood up to the director when working on the lights at the college rehearsal.

At the end of rehearsal, Roger had been waiting in the wings. "Stella," he said to Nanette in a knowing tone, "you are a damn fine actress." He was not tall or short but of average height, with broad shoulders and a barrel chest. He appeared capable of hoisting a full keg of beer up on a table.

"Oh," Nanette said as she felt her cheeks flush at the compliment. "Thank you." She started to walk off, but Roger gently took hold of her wrist in his big paw of a hand.

"I am going to shine the lights on you big time, pretty woman." His confident smile gleamed, and his thick eyebrows drew together over the bridge of his vast nose. It turned out that Roger was also from Bethesda but had attended a different high school than Nanette. "It is destiny," he told her. "Two Bethesdans who were meant to meet."

After that, Nanette could not refuse the advances of this bear of a man; he made her feel as though she were in the presence of the inevitable. Although attracted to Roger, she found his larger-than-life presence intimidating, but she kept getting drawn in deeper until, before she knew it, she was married in her senior year of college.

"Your sommelier has arrived."

"Oh," Nanette said, "I didn't see you coming."

Devin placed two bottles of wine on the table. "I brought a cabernet and a chardonnay."

Nanette smiled a knowing smile as she noted Devin in a turquoise polo shirt and tan khaki shorts.

"What?" Devin said.

"You are dressed just as I suspected." But she didn't suspect how stunning he would look, his tanned skin in perfect contrast to the light-blue shirt, or his clean-shaven face with his cheeks flushed with color. He looked like a model for Lands' End or L. L. Bean.

Devin held his open palms in front of his chest and gave himself a glance. "I'm a rather predictable fellow." He pulled back a chair across from Nanette and sat. He lifted the chardonnay. "I am going to guess the lady likes white wine." He lowered his brow, his dark blue eyes a-twinkle.

Nanette nodded. "We're even."

After Devin opened and poured the wine, he lifted his glass. "A toast to new beginnings."

Nanette clinked his glass as the moment sunk in. She was happy—not over-the-top happy but a comfortable at-ease sense of enjoying the company of a good man, a man she wanted to get to know, a man she wanted—*Slow down*, she told herself.

CHAPTER 14

DEVIN GAVE HIS GLASS OF wine a swish and took a swallow. It had a full-bodied taste that offered a smooth satisfaction. He leaned back and exchanged looks with Nanette, as the moment seemed upon them. He asked her how her wine was.

"I like it." She smiled her approval.

Another silence before Devin said, "How are you finding your new life in Pleasantville?"

"Pleasant." Nanette laughed.

They continued a small-talk conversation about the weather. "It can get scorching hot in the summer," Devin said.

"That's why God invented air conditioning," Nanette said. "I can take the heat but not the ice and snow." Her voice, lively with melodic contours, had an achy-breaky resonance.

"I hear you," Devin said, "though I do miss the brisk days of autumn."

As they sat and sipped on their wine, continuing the small talk, a mellow sense of well-being came over Devin. It was a feeling he hadn't felt in a good long while. Nanette's physical beauty in conjunction with her good-spirited humor drew him to want to be with her, to talk with her, to understand her.

"So," Devin said as he refilled Nanette's glass and then his, "who exactly is Nanette Brinson?"

"When I find out, I will let you know." Nanette offered a tight smile.

"I think we are usually the last to see ourselves as we truly are," Devin said. He reached for Nanette's hand, their fingers interlacing, her warm touch sending a charge through him. "Maybe together ..." Devin hesitated as he considered if he had overstepped.

"Together," Nanette said with a squeeze of Devin's hand, "we shall see what we shall see."

After they finished their second glass of wine, Nanette asked Devin if he could start the grill.

"Sure," Devin said. "What are we cooking?"

"Salmon."

"Why don't I cook it while you handle the rest," Devin said.

Nanette stood. "Sounds like a plan, Mr. Handyman."

"Ah," Devin said as he got up and headed for the grill. "The lady has a talent for rhyme with nary a hint of condemnation."

Nanette shined a smile at Devin in such a way that it was all in her eyes, which seemed aglow, as though a switch had been turned on.

During the meal, which was delicious—Nanette had prepped the salmon with a lemon sauce that was a perfect complement; the sweet potatoes and broccoli were fresh and seasoned just right; and the salad had a zesty, refreshing tang—the conversation at the kitchen table took on a different tone, as the light chitchat was replaced by each opening up a bit about themselves.

Nanette said that the one big what-if in her life was that she had stopped acting after college. "I should have at least done some local theater once my son was older."

"Well, you are making up for it, now that you are going to audition."

"Yes, but still," Nanette said as she forked a piece of fish and held it for a moment, as if considering. "What about you, Devin. Any what-ifs?"

Devin took a sip of his wine and looked out the kitchen window for a moment at the orange sun tottering on the azure horizon. "How long you got?" They exchanged looks for a beat before Devin said, "Never married, no children, no roots." He sunk his fork into his salad bowl and chomped down a mouthful of greens. "Good salad, by the way," he said in a wistful voice. He folded his hands under his chin, with his elbows on the table. "After Vietnam, it was hard to get that time out of my mind. The inhumanity that I saw—not only committed by the enemy but Americans too ..."

He returned his attention to his plate, cut a broccoli spear, and took a bite. "It seemed that a road trip was a way to escape the horrors of war." He felt a catch in his throat. "I've never talked about this, but it seems the road trip included my life's work that took up a good chunk of my life."

Nanette finished the last of her fish and leaned forward. "There is still time." She lifted her brow, her eyes saying, *Agreed?*

"Maybe," Devin said. "Maybe."

After Devin insisted on helping Nanette clear the table and do the dishes, he said, "I better get going—new job starting tomorrow."

Nanette walked Devin to the door.

"Thank you for not only a great meal but good company." Devin wanted to kiss her good night but held back. "I will see you Friday at, say, six? I'm kind of an early bird."

"Six it is." Nanette looked at Devin, and her eyes, which seemed to see things, had a look of expectation.

Devin leaned toward her, and she lifted her face to his. Her lips, so soft and heart-shaped, met his. Her scent filled Devin with wonder. It was fresh and clean, as one might find in a meadow of wildflowers. He lost himself in the moment, as though he was floating on a cloud of bliss, of promises, of good things to come.

CHAPTER 15

Nanette watched Devin drive off in his pickup and wondered if he would pick her up for their date in it—she hadn't seen another vehicle in his driveway when she had biked by. She had never ridden in a pickup and wasn't sure she liked the idea of rattling down the road in a smelly, dusty truck.

But she most certainly liked the idea of going out with Devin—to sit with him in a public setting, to people-watch and watch the people watching them, two beautiful people. She knew it was snobby to consider looks as a criterion for an attraction to someone, but it was the way of the world. And she also was being snobby in fretting about going out in a pickup. Weren't there more critical things with which to concern herself? *Unconventional* was a good word to describe this new man in her life, but was he in her life, and was she in his? Not yet—she hadn't been sure he would even kiss her good night.

This was her first date with a man other than her husband in forty years—forty! Seeping into her mind was the concern about a man who had lived a roaming life, never settling down. He had most likely had relationships with women along the way, breaking them off when he went on to his next town. Did he love them and leave them, or was it a mutual separation? Nanette did not want to fall for Devin only to have him break it off with her. *"Sorry, Nanette, but I don't want to get in too deep. Maybe we need a break and then see."*

And was she ready for a relationship so soon after Roger's passing? Was she not looking forward to some independence in her life, a go-it-alone lifestyle and see how it suited her?

Nanette shoved her concerns on the back burner as she tried to imagine how the date would go—drinks and dinner and then what?

Back to her place and … Would he come on to her, and if so, how far would she let it go. Only one man had ever seen her naked, and the thought of undressing in front of Devin caused her to cringe. It seemed like an invasion of privacy. *I'm a shy snob,* she told herself as she turned from the window.

Nanette checked her email and found a reply from the local theater that her audition for the part of Amanda Wingfield was next Wednesday at five. A nervous tingle ran down her spine and settled in the pit of her stomach. Further down the notice, she was given the lines she would be rehearsing. It was the scene where Amanda regales her two children with tales of her idyllic youth and the scores of suitors who once pursued her.

Amanda was a well-meaning but overbearing parent to her two adult children. Her husband had deserted her, and she found herself faced with an empty and meaningless life that triggered illusions of her past and present lives. Nanette felt confident that she could portray this character.

She needed to memorize her lines—she wanted to do the audition without a script—and also work on a Southern accent, just enough to hint at the faded Southern belle.

Nanette's last performance was in *A Streetcar Named Desire,* as Stella, who was a calm, reasonable foil to her sister, Blanche, a mentally fragile and narcissistic woman. She had played Stella with an upper-class Southern accent, accentuated by clear, distinct pronunciations.

Never had Nanette felt more alive than when on the stage performing as Stella. It had been an exhausting but thrilling experience. She had to juggle schoolwork, the play, and the arrival of her future husband, who had pursued her with spellbinding efficiency.

On their first date at the Italian restaurant, Roger said, "Stella's character must show contrast to kooky Blanche." He settled his intense gaze on Nanette, his deep-set eyes drawing her attention. "Where Blanche is flighty, Stella must show her dignity of bearing."

Nanette took that advice and ran with it, always projecting on stage an air of calm to Blanche's dizziness.

It was as though during this period of heightened sensitivity to her stage presence, Nanette's real-life presence was inexplicably drawn to

Roger, the lighting technician, who wooed Nanette with a confident certitude, as though their future together was a given.

If she had met Roger at a later period in her life, would she still have been pulled into his orbit without the connection of the play, where Roger cast light on her, both literally and figuratively, or would Nanette have thought of him as an overbearing know-it-all?

Nanette turned her attention back to the present. With the character of Amanda, she thought an occasional uncertain tremble in her voice would add a bit of authenticity. But not too much—just enough to reveal the faded Southern belle she had become.

She got a notepad and pen from a kitchen drawer, returned to her laptop at the kitchen nook, and began writing out her lines. A fellow thespian in college had mentioned that he always wrote out his lines by hand. "Because your brain holds on to information better after you've written it down."

She then took her laptop into the office and printed out the scene.

Back in the kitchen, she put the printed scene on the countertop and began her first self-rehearsal.

Nanette cleared her throat and began speaking her lines as she sank into the character of Amanda Wingfield. *There you go*, Nanette told herself. She felt a rush of inspiration, as though an old friend had returned after a very long absence.

CHAPTER 16

D EVIN GOT HOME FROM WORK, showered and shaved, and went to his closet. He wanted to wear shorts and a polo shirt for his date with Nanette, but he decided on khaki trousers; a button-down, short-sleeved dark blue shirt; and a pair of penny loafers with no socks. He hadn't worn those shoes in nearly two years, not since his last date. Clothes were not Devin's strong suit—or more correctly, not a major concern. He was most comfortable in a T-shirt and shorts.

But he had a strong sense that Nanette was more of a traditionalist in this regard, and he needed to at least be not too far off her level of dress. He had made reservations at Norma's, a trendy place in town with an outdoor seating area. Not a place he would frequent, but he thought sitting outside at a table would suit Nanette.

Oh shoot, Devon thought. Last time he had taken a woman on a date, he'd had a sedan, but he'd sold it a year earlier since it was just taking up space. He did not want to take her in his pickup, and he didn't think she would be all that pleased if he did, though she probably wouldn't show it. He thought about a taxi but immediately nixed it—too un-Devin like. He could walk to her house, and they could walk the mile into town from her place. Or he could ride his bike to her house, and she could decide to ride bikes, or he could drive her car.

"You're a piece of work, McCortland," Devin said aloud as he gave himself one last look in the mirror over his dresser. *She might as well know what she's dealing with before this thing gets too far along*, he thought as he headed for the door.

Devin kept his bike in the backyard in a bike rack he had built. There were two other bikes that he had bought at a yard sale, thinking guests might use them at some point, but there were no takers yet.

His bike was a twenty-year-old Schwinn mountain hybrid that was perfect. It had wide handlebars so he didn't have to lean forward and a basket in front that he used to carry beer or a few items at the grocery store. The height and length of the bike fit his body just right.

He had purchased the bike on a job in La Crosse, Wisconsin, when a woman he was seeing was into biking. Her name was Brenda, and she was the closest Devin had come to a serious relationship since Manhattan Beach. Brenda and Devin had a lot in common: they both liked any form of exercise; she dressed casually—shorts or jeans and a T-shirt or flannel shirt and no makeup; and she was down-to-earth. At the time, Devin was forty-four, and Brenda was thirty-six and divorced with a ten-year-old son, with whom Devin developed a relationship through a common interest in sports. Depending on the season, they played catch, shot hoops, or tossed the football.

At the end of Devin's job in La Crosse, he needed to make a decision. Did he want to settle down in La Crosse and marry Brenda? He wasn't sure what her answer would be. They were fond of each other but not madly in love. If he had worked full time in La Crosse, he thought he might have done it and established roots. But the call of the road—that restless spirit inside Devin—encouraged departure.

Even so, he wasn't sure that Brenda wanted to get married. She had a good life—she was active in the community, volunteered for the Red Cross, helped with triathlons and other races, and had a good-paying job for the county. But Brenda made it easy for Devin. On their last date, with his departure the next day, she told him that she had enjoyed their time together and, as if reading his mind, that he had nothing to feel guilty about. "Maybe if we'd met at another point in our lives, marriage might have been an option." They were at a local brew pub, in a booth, drinking drafts. "But as with most things in life"—Brenda lifted her mug and took a long swallow—"timing is everything."

CHAPTER 17

NANETTE HAD MEMORIZED HER AUDITION lines as Amanda Wingfield. She had the accent to a level at which she was comfortable—not too much high-pitched twang but enough to let the listener know that her character was a well-bred Southern woman but with angst.

She had studied her scene, repeated her lines while standing at the kitchen counter, and then, in her head, reacted to the other character's lines. She also watched a 1950 version of *The Glass Menagerie* with Gertrude Lawrence, an accomplished British actress, playing Amanda. Nanette noted how she delivered her lines with a sort of rushed anxiety, but when she reminisced about her glorious youth and gentleman callers, her voice and body movement calmed down.

Nanette had her own gentleman caller arriving soon. She stood in front of her mirror, deciding what to wear. If they were going out in Devin's pickup, a dress didn't seem appropriate. She picked clamdiggers and a blue-and-white striped long-sleeved blouse that didn't hide the natural curves of her body. *Not bad,* she thought. *Not bad at all for a woman your age.*

A few years back at a neighborhood Fourth of July block party, Nanette and a neighbor were standing next to a keg set up in the street. While the man poured himself a beer, he said under his breath to Nanette, "There are women twenty years younger than you, right here this evening, who would *kill* to look like you." He then offered Nanette a pronounced wink and wobbled off.

Nanette picked up a small bottle of rose essential oils she had bought for her date. She studied it for a moment and then dabbed a drop on the back of each wrist; she started for behind her ear but stopped. She put the oil away and went into the living room to wait for Devin.

The chimes of the doorbell surprised Nanette. She had not heard Devin's pickup arrive. She answered the door.

"Hi," Devin said through a rueful smile. "I rode my bike over."

"Oh," Nanette said as she waved Devin inside the foyer. "What's the plan?"

"Did you ever watch *Let's Make a Deal?*"

"Monty Hall." Nanette wasn't sure where this was going, but Devin had piqued her interest. "Do we need to sit down?"

"No," Devin replied. "Door number one is, I drive your car to our destination." He slanted an inquiring look at Nanette. "Norma's, in town, is a little over a mile from here."

"Oh," Nanette said. She remembered the restaurant she had seen when she first arrived in town; it had a cozy outdoor dining area along the walkway. "Let me guess," she said through a *a-ha* smile. "Door number two is we ride bikes into town, and door number three is we walk." She made a face. *Am I right?*

"Oh boy," Devin said as he rubbed the back of his neck, "I see I am in the midst of a woman who has already figured me out."

"I say we ride our bikes," Nanette said.

"Perfect," Devin said with a confirming nod.

Devin locked their bikes at a bike rack in front of the post office, and they walked down Main Street to the restaurant. All the outdoor tables were full, so they sat on two-corner stools at the U-shaped bar.

"Folks," the bartender said, "what may I get you?" He was an older man, probably a retiree, with thinning white hair, pink cheeks, and a friendly way about him.

Devin turned to Nanette. "Chablis?"

Nanette glanced at the bar with bottles of liquor stacked in front of a plate-glass mirror. "Vodka tonic," she said to the bartender.

"Make that two," Devin said, lifting two fingers.

When the drinks arrived, Devin lifted his to Nanette. "A toast," he said as he clinked Nanette's glass, "to adventure and change."

Nanette took a sip, placed her drink on the bar, and ran her finger over the rim. "I believe you just paraphrased a line from *The Glass Menagerie.*"

"I never forgot that line after I saw the play all those years back." Devin removed his lime from the side of his glass and squeezed it into his drink, causing a fizzy reaction of tiny bubbles that rose to the surface. "It seemed an accurate description of my life back then—that is, for one looking at it from the outside. Inside, though, it was more of an illusion, and if memory serves me, that is at the heart of the play—illusion."

Nanette felt the thrumming impact of corporeal desire. This man had depth; this man, she wanted.

By the time they finished their drinks, an outdoor corner table was available. Devin sat with his back to the street. Nanette ordered another vodka tonic, and Devin, a draft beer.

"How many places have you lived in during your career?" Nanette asked.

Devin leaned back as their server, a young Latino who identified himself as Jose, served Nanette her cocktail and Devin his beer. Devin nodded a thank-you and lifted his mug by the handle. He took a long, thirsty swallow and squinted to get his focus. "Fifteen, including Pleasantville."

"I'm the opposite," Nanette said with a lift of her brow, as though to say, *That's the way it is.* "Two homes within three miles of each other and now here."

"Think this is your last?"

Nanette's bottom lip pouched out. "Part of me still can't believe I am actually here," she said in a considering tone. "My son, whom I told you about, would like me to consider moving to New Zealand if Florida doesn't work out."

Devin's eyes met Nanette's. A look passed over his face of one hearing unexpected and disappointing news. He recovered quickly and said, "What made you decide to move?"

Nanette removed the lime from the rim of her drink and placed it carefully on the table. "Besides my son, my older sister is my only remaining family. She's married and living in London with two grown children, who are British citizens." She took a swallow of her drink and looked at Devin. "There was nothing to keep me in Maryland, other than a few friends and memories of ..." Nanette stared off for a moment. "I thought a change of scenery was necessary." She lifted her hands, palms facing Devin, indicating *enough said*. "What about you? Is this your last home?"

"Yes," Devin replied. "I've moved enough to last ten lifetimes." He cradled his mug, took a swallow, and wiped his mouth with the back of his forefinger. "For better or worse, this is my last stop."

The dinner was succulent. Devin had broiled scallops with asparagus and tangy coleslaw. Nanette had mahi-mahi with mashed sweet potatoes and the house salad. For dessert, she suggested they share a slice of chocolate cheesecake. "I have an incurable sweet tooth," she said through a guilty smile.

By the time they got to their bikes at the post office, dusk was upon them. Devin turned on his bike's rear and front lights and told Nanette to go first, and he would follow.

"I'm going to put lights on your bike," Devin said as they headed out, "before our next—" He hesitated, not wanting to get ahead of himself.

Nanette glanced over her shoulder. "Before our next date—if I may finish your sentence."

"Like I said"—Devin laughed—"you have me figured out."

CHAPTER 18

O N THE RIDE BACK, NANETTE stayed a couple of bike lengths ahead of Devin, who rode at a slow pace. It had been an enjoyable time, drinking and eating and talking with this man who had lived such a peripatetic life. Over dinner, Devin had talked about the pleasure he got after finishing a big job, whether a highway, a bridge, an irrigation project, or any other structure or pathway that needed to be built. "There was a certain joyful sadness at the end," Devin had told Nanette. "Joy to have completed a solid job and sadness at having to uproot myself and start all over again—not just a new job but a new world to live in."

Nanette thought that *joyful sadness* was an apt description of Devin. Outwardly, he projected a confident, good-to-go demeanor, but there were instances where his cover was blown, when a look of regret flashed over his face when talking about his past, as some staggered memory seemed to have resurfaced, before his expression returned to the present.

As they came onto Nanette's street, she had a decision to make. Of course, she would invite Devin inside, but would he make an advance toward her, and if so, how far was she willing to go? Physically, she wanted to lie naked with him, to caress him, to make passionate love to him. But the mental side, the woman who had been with only one man in her entire life, hesitated at the prospect of such a daring leap.

When they got off their bikes in the driveway, Nanette said, "Would like to come in and have a drink on the back patio?"

"I'd like that," Devin said as he offered his hand for Nanette to lead the way.

In the kitchen, Nanette said, "I bought a six-pack of Coors." She scrunched up her face, eyes on Devin.

"When I left Manhattan Beach, back in the day, I spent a couple of days in Boulder, backdropped by the Rockies, and left with six cases of Coors—love that beer."

"Well, then," Nanette said, "let's make it a cold beer for you and a cold beer for me." She offered her hand to the refrigerator. "You grab two bottles—let's skip glasses—and exit, stage left, to the patio, while I turn on the outdoor lights."

After they sat at the wrought-iron table, Nanette took a sniff of her beer and found it had a malty, grainy smell. She took a sip, smacked her lips, and took a swig. "Not bad," she said to Devin, who had an appreciative grin plastered across his face.

"Watch out," Devin teased. "Next thing, you'll be drinking boilermakers."

They settled back into a comfortable silence, drinking their beers, as the moon slid up the blue-black sky awash in twinkling stars.

By the time Nanette had finished her beer, a calm had settled over her—a calm that told her not to be afraid but to let the inevitable happen.

Making love with Devin was heaven on earth; his body was packed with lean, sinewy muscle. It was so different from heavyset Roger, whose style was wham-bam-thank-you-ma'am, roll over and out of bed.

Afterward, Devin and Nanette lay in bed face-to-face, staring into each other's eyes in a silent absorption.

"I'd like to get to know you," Devin said in a singsong voice.

Nanette tapped Devin's nose and smiled. "And me, you."

"Promise me one thing."

"Anything."

"You won't go on your way," Devin said in a more serious voice.

"I promise."

CHAPTER 19

A FTER A SECOND SESSION OF lovemaking, Devin decided that he didn't want to overstay his welcome and rode his bike back home. But not before he had volunteered to get lights at the bike shop for Nanette's bike and put them on the following day, after which they could take a bike ride, followed by lunch on her patio.

Sex with Nanette had been most pleasurable—her body was supple, skin smooth as silk, breasts full and firm. Along with her beauty was a keen and perceptive mind that seemed to see things. Her comment that it might have been a blessing that it didn't work out with Gretchen was spot-on. Had he been running from that loss, rambling from town to town, building and repairing for all those years? Deep down, he knew it was more than that.

Vietnam had done a number on Devin, traveling from locale to locale, building and rebuilding blown-up bridges and structures, all while witnessing the horrors of war—the native people's lives turned upside down in such a senseless conflict, comrades dying, enemies killed, some just children.

There was a joint venture with Navy SEALs in repairing a bridge; sniper fire took the lives of one SEAL and wounded two others. Their leader, a young lieutenant, took a team on a night patrol and returned at dawn, gripping the severed head of a Vietnamese boy, no more than twelve years old. "The only good gook is a dead gook," were the lieutenant's words.

"You son of a bitch!" Devin shouted, charging the lieutenant as weapons were drawn—army versus navy. "Drop the head!" Devin stood eyeball-to-eyeball with this murderous thug.

"Hell, no," the lieutenant said, spittle spraying out of his mouth and onto Devin's face. "We're gonna mount gook-boy on a stake as a warning."

"Over my dead body," Devin said. He turned his attention to the SEALs, with their weapons drawn. "Which one of you bastards is going to shoot me, huh?" He was ready to die, if need be, but that boy's head was going to get buried.

"You're crazier than we are," the lieutenant said as he dropped the head.

Returning to the States from an unpopular war—Devin's mind was a blur, save his vivid flashbacks of the war—falling in love with Gretchen, and then her leaving seemed to precipitate Devin's controlled wanderlust.

Now, at a later stage in his life, Devin had met a woman. Nanette had a certain physical beauty and grace about her that was, in some ways, like an older version of Gretchen. And Nanette had drawn Devin in like no woman had since Gretchen. He didn't want to look too far down the road, but Devin would be more than a little pleased to spend a good long while in the company of Nanette Brinson.

CHAPTER 20

D EVIN ARRIVED AT NANETTE'S DRIVEWAY on his bike at ten on the dot with a red taillight and a front light in his basket, along with a toolbox. In fifteen minutes, he had both lights installed, and then he showed Nanette how to turn them off and on. "I always keep the taillight on whenever I ride," he said as he turned his on.

Nanette turned her taillight on. "Where are we riding?"

"There's a park trail not far that is a fifteen-mile loop around a lake." Devin lifted an inquiring brow.

"Is it hilly?"

"Not a lot of hills in Florida."

"OK, then," Nanette said. "Sounds like a plan." She thought herself in good enough shape, having taken up walking and exercise classes in the last few years at the YMCA in Bethesda.

The bike ride on the Seminole Trail was more fun than Nanette could remember. The ride was at an easy pace, with multiple stops at trailside overlooks, where they saw alligators basking on the banks of the lake, as well as heron, beaver, and various birds chirping and dodging in and out of the pine and shrub trees.

At each stop, Devin pointed out something of interest. "Hear that?" he said, cocking his head. "Look up to your left."

Nanette peered up to the source of a knocking sound and saw a big, dashing bird with a flaming crest, pecking into the trunk of a tree. "It looks like an overgrown woodpecker."

"Pileated woodpecker. It's excavating insects."

"Excavating?" Nanette teased. "You sound like you're back on one of your big projects."

Without missing a beat, Devin said, "You can excavate the boy from the big job, but you can't excavate the big job from the boy."

Back at Nanette's, they ate tuna salad on rye with lettuce, tomato, and mayo, with a vinaigrette salad that Devin said was *delish*.

After they did the dishes, Devin asked Nanette if she would like to come by his house for dinner. "Shrimp on the barbie, corn on the cob, and—" Devin wiped his hands on a paper towel, squinting as though trying to decide.

"I'll make a complementary salad," Nanette said.

Devin offered to come by and escort her, but she declined. "I'll stow my fixings in my bike's basket. What time?"

They agreed on six.

Devin's house was of similar size to Nanette's but with a bare-bones quality that screamed for a woman's touch. There were the appropriate furnishings but no photos or family mementos, just a few prints of Florida fauna on the walls; there was nothing that said anything about the occupant.

But what the house lacked in touches was more than made up for by a multisided wood deck in Devin's backyard. It was elevated off the ground and surrounded by a post and picket railing. In a corner octagon was a stone firepit with benches along the railing. Closer to the sliding door entrance was a sitting area with Adirondack chairs and a ship captain's table. On the other side, near the house, was an L-shaped stone bar with a granite countertop, equipped with a barbeque grill and high-back chairs. And across from the bar, next to the railing, were a red cedar table and four matching deck chairs. To top it off, there were running lights on the deck, along the perimeter.

"Did you make all this?" Nanette asked with a sweep of her hand.

"I did." Devin looked over his creation and settled his gaze on the Adirondack chairs. "Shall we?"

Devon asked if she would like anything to drink before dinner.

Nanette opted for ginger ale. "I had a bit too much last night," she added.

"I'll join you in ginger ales all around," Devin said from the bar, as he poured it into tall glasses of ice.

As they sat at the ship captain's table across from each other, Nanette asked Devin how hot it got in the summer in Pleasantville.

"Hot and humid, to say the least," Devin replied. He looked off for a moment. "But nothing compared to Vietnam—that was the hottest, most doggone humid place ..." His voice trailed off as he seemed to have caught himself.

Nanette wasn't sure if she should pursue the subject but decided to chance it. "How bad was it over there?"

Devin focused a strong beam of attention on Nanette. "One of my men was an English lit major from New York City," Devin said as his voice took on a wistful tone. "He would recite a poem every morning. It became a routine—the squad would gather in a circle around Corporal Henley, who had a deep, commanding voice."

"A specific poem or a variety?" Nanette asked.

Devin nodded, his face unchanged. "Specific, very specific—every one of us remembered it word for word—and I imagine every man still does to this day."

"What was the poem?"

"'Invictus' from the nineteenth century—1875 to be exact."

"I'm not familiar with it," Nanette said.

Devin began:

> Out of the night that covers me,
> Black as the pit from pole to pole,
> I thank whatever gods may be
> For my unconquerable soul.

Devin's voice had taken on a deep resonance, as though he were conjuring up the voice of his former corporal.

> In the fell clutch of circumstance
> I have not winced nor cried aloud.
> Under the bludgeoning of chance
> My head is bloody, but unbowed.

> Beyond this place of wrath and tears
> Looms but the Horror of the shade,
> And yet the menace of the years
> Finds, and shall find me, unafraid.

Devin's words were strong and clear but wracked with the intensity of his experience.

> It matters not how strait the gate,
> How charged with punishments the scroll,
> I am the master of my fate:
> I am the captain of my soul.

Devin lifted his brow as a faint smile seemed to come to his eyes. "After his recital, Henley would look up into the jungle foliage, as if searching, and say with utter gratitude, 'Thank you, Great Uncle Ernest, for your words of inspiration that will get us through this difficult time.'"

Nanette looked at Devin, a question in her eyes.

"Henley claimed," Devin said with a shrug, "that the poet was his great-grandfather's brother—William Ernest Henley, famous back in his time." Devin shrugged again. "But I will tell you, Nanette, that it helped. So"—Devin suddenly changed his tone, a tone that said, *New subject*—"are you excited about your audition?"

Nanette grimaced in mock fear. "Yes, and a little nervous, to say the least."

"Prediction," Devin said with finger raised. "You will not only get the part but give a great performance."

"And," Nanette said, slanting an inquisitive look across the table, "you know this because?"

"Because," Devin said with an affirming nod, "I know great talent when I see it."

CHAPTER 21

N ANETTE ARRIVED EARLY FOR HER audition and stood in the back of
the Pleasantville Theater, which had a bare-bones setup. A man and
two women were sitting in folding chairs in front of a raised wooden
stage with curtains drawn. Nanette assumed it was the directorial staff.

On the stage, a young man in a white shirt, with long sleeves rolled
to the elbows, and wearing suspenders, stood facing the audience of
three.

"Whenever you're ready," the man seated said with a flourishing
wave of his hand.

The actor began reading his lines.

Nanette was impressed by the strong, confident delivery as the
young man sank into the character of Tom Wingfield, Amanda's son.
As she gave her lines one last look, Nanette perked up as the actor, in
character, mentioned turning back time.

That line struck Nanette. Was she trying to turn back time by
auditioning after all these years? She had definitely turned back time in
regards to her romance with Devin. She felt like an infatuated schoolgirl
with her first crush.

They had spent the weekend together—dinner at his place on
Saturday, followed by biking the short distance back to her place, each
with their lights on. Devin spent the night, and he left early Sunday
morning, promising to check in later. "I have to get a few things squared
away for a concrete pad I'm pouring first thing Monday morning," he
explained. "I was supposed to do it yesterday, but something *came* up."

"Do I detect a fellow thespian with that sly pun, Sir Devin?"
Nanette was lying in bed, chin on her palm.

Now, Nanette's attention was drawn up front, where another young man was called to the stage and performed the same reading of Tom's character.

After another audition for Tom, the director said, in a *ta-da* voice, "And our last audition—Nanette Brinson."

"Yes," Nanette said with a raise of her hand.

The director, who was in his early sixties, balding, with slouched shoulders and a seen-it-all look about him, waved Nanette to come forward.

She had thought about buying a period-piece dress appropriate for the South in the late thirties but decided it too forward. Instead, she wore a white blouse with a frilly collar, pencil skirt, and a pair of white slip-on canvas shoes. She knew the outfit was a bit off, but she thought it fit the character.

Up the three steps and onto center stage. It felt good to be back, if a bit nerve-racking. Nanette took a deep breath and told herself it was like riding a bike.

"Let's see," the director said, scanning a clipboard. He looked up, a thin smile spreading across his face as he took in the woman on stage before him. He nodded approvingly. "Uh-huh, you're trying out for Amanda." He looked at the woman to his right, "Joyce, would you go up and read the other characters' lines."

CHAPTER 22

Devin rode his bike to the post office and locked it with Nanette's at the bike rack. He told himself to get her a bike-chain lock. The plan was to meet outside the restaurant at six, but Nanette hadn't shown, so he decided to slip into the theater. He wasn't sure if this would upset her—his watching her audition—so he peeked in the doorway and saw Nanette standing on stage with a woman holding a script.

Devin eased his way over into the back shadows of the structure. It had been a library before a new one was built back in the nineties at another site.

An overhead light shone softly down on Nanette as she stood on stage. As she began her performance, somehow Nanette transformed herself into Amanda Wingfield. She had an expression of overbearing righteousness, her stance was erect, her eyes were two beads of concentration, and her lovely, heart-shaped mouth was twisted into an oddly naked look. It came over Devin that the woman before him on the stage was an actress. It was in her bones, in her being. The fact that she had neglected this talent for forty years …

Nanette flicked her hands out and turned sharply as she fell into the rhythm of the lines. As she continued her audition, the director leaned forward in his chair, as if ready to spring from his seat.

He glanced at the woman sitting next to him, his expression that of finding a new discovery. When Nanette finished, the director stood. "Ms. Brinson," he said in an excited tone, "may I call you Nanette?"

Nanette smiled and nodded as she seemed to untangle herself from Amanda Wingfield; her body and face uncoiled from the tense erectness she had maintained on stage.

"Nanette," the director said, splaying his hands out to the side, "rehearsals begin next Monday. I look forward to working with you."

CHAPTER 23

WHEN THE DIRECTOR TOLD NANETTE he looked forward to working with her, it didn't register at first that she had won the part. She felt her bottom lip drop before recovering.

He went on to tell Nanette, "Rehearsals are Monday, Wednesday, and Friday, with TBAs from time to time."

Nanette squinted a questioning look. "TBAs?"

"To be announced," the director said. "I expect all my actors to put this production at the top of their to-do lists."

Is this really happening? Nanette thought as she seemed to float down the stage steps and over to the director, who introduced himself and his two assistants.

She was then given a packet with a schedule for rehearsals, a standard resident theater contract, and a copy of the script.

As Nanette departed the theater, she was still trying to comprehend what had just taken place. She knew it was unusual for an actor to be offered a part after the first audition; often there were callbacks and a waiting period before finding out. She thought she had given a strong performance as Amanda Wingfield, and she could tell by the manner in which the director had reacted to her performance that she had made a big impression. It felt so good to have her talent recognized, a talent she was not even sure she still possessed. The performance itself had been as though a current of some strong different life had swept through her.

Outside the theater, she regained her bearings. *Oh yes*, she thought as she saw Devin. They were going to Norma's.

"I have a confession," Devin said.

"You watched my audition." Nanette heard the excitement in her voice.

Devin put his hand on her shoulder, and in his eyes, Nanette saw an attentiveness and a kind of newfound respect. "You were Amanda Wingfield. You knocked it out of the park."

A sense of accomplishment settled over Nanette as they walked toward the restaurant. Devin took her hand in his. And with that sense of accomplishment, there was another sense that from here on out, her life, as she knew it, was headed in a new and unknown direction.

CHAPTER 24

THERE WERE SEATS AVAILABLE OUTSIDE at Norma's, but Nanette asked Devin if they could eat inside.

"Sure," he said.

Inside, Nanette asked for a table for two in a back corner. After they were seated, Nanette requested water. "I want to study the script when I get home tonight," she said to Devin.

"Make that two waters," Devin said to their server, who then handed out menus and gave the specials for the night.

Devin had been looking forward to a couple of beers, a fine meal, and lovemaking back at Nanette's, but he realized that change was in the air—that the play was now front and center in Nanette's mind.

"We have rehearsals three days a week," Nanette said with a rise in her voice. "And last-minute rehearsals—to be announced."

When their waters arrived, Devin asked if Nanette wanted an appetizer.

"I'm ready to order," she said to the waiter.

Whoa, Devin thought, as he felt an uneasiness come over him.

Devin had walked into town and drove Nanette home in her car. At her front door, he said, "I know you are anxious to get to your script—"

"Thank you," Nanette said in a hurried, relieved voice. "It's all a bit overwhelming."

A silent pause hung in the air before Devin said, "Well, good night." He lifted his hand in farewell.

Nanette leaned into Devin and planted a kiss on his cheek. "Call me in a couple days?" She squinted at him.

"Will do." He turned and stepped off the front stoop.

On the walk home, Devin pondered a new suitor in Nanette's life—the stage.

By Friday morning, Devin had not heard from Nanette and decided to give her a call. "How's the studying going?"

"I'm getting there," Nanette said.

"How about dinner at my place tonight, including me making the salad? All the first lady of the theater has to do is show up?"

"Ha-ha."

"Well?"

"Yes, that would be nice," Nanette said. "Say, six, Mr. Early Bird?"

After hanging up, Devin realized he had to get a move on. He was on a job for Ed Feldman that had to be finished today. It was a vacant home that Ed was showing to a prospective buyer the next day. Devin had to fix a leaky toilet, replace the faulty garbage disposal, and attend to a couple of other minor details.

He methodically went about his work. He replaced the toilet flapper and muscled out the old garbage disposal and installed the new one, all while contemplating his dinner. Multitasking was a skill that Devin had applied in Vietnam and in his career. This was on a much smaller level but important, though no one's life was at stake.

So take your time and see it through, he told himself.

Grilled chicken with asparagus and a Caesar salad would work, he thought as he went to his truck to retrieve a bucket of paint.

By four thirty, Devin had finished all his tasks and zipped off to the grocery store. He got home, took a shower, shaved, and changed into a polo shirt and Bermuda shorts. *Oh, my God,* he thought. He had forgotten to buy white wine for Nanette. He checked the time—fifteen minutes to six. He hustled out the front door and got home right at six with a bottle of white and a bottle of red.

By six fifteen, Devin had marinated the chicken and was prepping the asparagus when the front doorbell rang.

"Sorry, I'm late," Nanette said with a little shrug. "I bought a bottle of white wine, just in case you forgot."

"I did," Devin said, "but I remembered in the nick of time."

"Ha," Nanette said through a big grin, "I knew it."

Devin lifted his chin toward Nanette's bike in the driveway. "I see you are getting into the Pleasantville lifestyle."

"I have a good guide," Nanette said with a nod toward Devin, as if to confirm her words.

They went out to the back deck with glasses of wine in hand.

"Let's sit at the bar," Nanette said.

"Sure," Devin said. He thought her voice had a happy ring to it. She seemed like her old self; the tension in her voice and demeanor from the other night after her audition was gone.

They sat, and Devin swiveled in his stool so that he was facing Nanette. "So, how is the studying of the script going?"

"I am *still* working on memorizing all my lines," Nanette said. She took a sip of her wine and smiled at Devin. "It's scary-exciting."

"You'll do great," Devin said. "You have what it takes."

"I had it," Nanette said. She placed her elbow on the bar and rested her chin in the palm of her hand. "The question is, do I still have it."

They ate at the red cedar table on the deck. The dinner turned out to be a hit—Nanette loved all of it. "My handyman is handy in the kitchen also, I see."

Nanette volunteered to help with cleanup, but Devin splayed his hands out at the empty plates, bowls and platters of remaining food, and cutlery. "I'm going to worry about all that tomorrow. How about another glass of wine for the lady, and then I'll let you have your way with me?"

"Can we head over to my place for the wine?" Nanette offered an inquisitive smile. "And," she said in a singsong voice, "hank-kee-pank-kee." Her smile widened and her brow lifted, as if to say, *Whadda you think?*

"Wine and hanky-panky at your place, it is."

On Saturday morning, Devin and Nanette took a bike ride in the park, stopping along the way to observe the wildlife, but Nanette's cheery mood from the previous day was replaced by a different demeanor—if not sullen, then anticipatory—as though she was back to concentrating on the play.

It was as though she had allowed herself a twelve-hour liberty yesterday before kicking herself back into actress mode.

They took a break at a spot with a clear view of the lake, which was quiet, with nary a hint of wildlife.

"Favor," Nanette said in a pensive voice.

"Yes," Devin said.

"I'd like to get back home and study my lines for the opening rehearsal on Monday."

Devin was struck, as always, by her reticent beauty, as though behind the lovely façade, secrets were being formulated. "Why don't I call you on Tuesday after your first rehearsal, and we go from there?"

Nanette smiled as though pleased at the suggestion. Her eyes gave Devin a look of gratitude.

For the first time, he saw the depth of her acting skills.

On Tuesday morning after Nanette's first rehearsal, Devin texted her to get together, but she replied, "Rehearsals are a long and slow grind. The director, John F'ing Abbot—that's what my fellow cast members call him—is a perfectionist. Can I get a raincheck?"

"Maybe this weekend?" Devin texted back.

"Saturday should work."

Part of Devin was upset with himself for practically begging, but the other, stronger part did not want her out of his life.

He sank himself into his work to take his mind off fretting. He gave out estimates at discount prices on the spot, just to ensure he would stay busy. And busy he was, as he replaced an old, decrepit post-and-rail fence with a picket fence, digging the post holes and sinking the posts in concrete. He finished the job in a day and a half, then assembled and installed an arched cedar arbor at another job, followed by a string of small jobs: fixing a leaky kitchen faucet, replacing a broken window, and installing a security light over a garage and patching cracks in the driveway.

On Friday evening, Devin retired to his back deck, cold beer in hand. He was tempted to call Nanette—he had not heard a word from her—but he wasn't sure if she had finished rehearsal. *Give her a call tomorrow morning,* he told himself as he leaned back and watched the sun slide down the sky, showing through the tail of a silver cloud.

On Saturday morning at nine, Devin called Nanette and got her voice recording. "Hi, Nanette, how about a bike ride sometime this weekend?" Devin said in an easy-as-you-go tone. "Give me a call."

By ten o'clock, he hadn't heard and decided to take a ride to the park and do a double-lap around the lake.

After one lap, his phone rang. "Hello, Ms. Garbo," Devin said.

"Hi," Nanette said in a tentative voice.

"I'm at the lake, watching Mr. Beaver sunning himself on the bank."

"Ah," Nanette said.

"Look, Nanette, if you're tied up with the play and all—"

"No," Nanette said. "I want to see you." She went on to say that the rehearsal had gone on late last night. "The director installed some changes in how he wants me to approach my character."

"How about I pick up food and some wine, and I come over to your place?"

"That's a wonderful idea," Nanette said with an uptick in her voice. "Say, six, Mr. Early Bird?"

Later that day, Devin went to the liquor store and then to the grocery store, where he bought two pounds of shrimp, salad fixings, and a baguette. He made an arugula salad with red onion, Kalamata olives, cherry tomatoes, and red peppers. He mixed a honey-garlic marinade with the shrimp in a bowl and stored the contents in a Ziploc plastic bag. He then loaded the food in a knapsack, along with the wine and a corkscrew, and rode off on his bike.

At Nanette's house, Devin walked around to the back. He removed the knapsack from his shoulders, unloaded the two bottles of wine on the wrought-iron table, and opened both with the corkscrew. At the sliding glass door, he saw Nanette standing in the kitchen with her back to him, speaking in an animated voice. She was rehearsing. Devin tapped on the glass, startling Nanette, as her shoulders gave a sudden twitch.

She turned and threw a big smile at Devin, who opened the door. "Amanda Wingfield, I presume," he said.

"Oh!" Nanette laughed as she flashed her hands over her face. "She has left. Nanette, here."

It seemed Nanette had gotten so involved in studying and rehearsing her lines that she had forgotten the time. This seemed so unlike her. But this play had taken a grip on her and must have rekindled a long-lost passion. Devin imagined that every waking hour she was either at rehearsal or studying and practicing her lines.

"Rehearsals a grind?" he asked.

"The director, John Abbot, is a taskmaster but very knowledgeable," Nanette said with an arch of her brow, as though to confirm her words. "Not only about *The Glass Menagerie*—he wrote an article for a local paper about the play mirroring the life of the author—but the craft of acting."

It seemed the process had flipped on a switch inside Nanette, and her thespian switch appeared hard to turn off. She said that she went to bed thinking about the play, dreamed about Amanda, and woke up thinking about the nuances of her character. "I realize I need to keep a balance, but darn if it isn't hard." It was as though she was trying to make up for the forty years of dormancy.

"I left the wine on the table," Devin said with a lift of his head over his shoulder.

Nanette glanced down at her T-shirt, shorts, and flip-flops, giving herself the once-over. "Ah," she said through a slight grimace. "I should change."

"No," Devin said. "Grab a wine glass, go sit out back, and pour yourself a Chablis. I will prep dinner and then join you."

"You're too good to me," Nanette said. She came up to Devin, kissed him on the cheek, and smiled.

Devin watched her walk out to the patio table, sit, and take a swallow of her wine. She leaned back in her chair, her expression seeming to say, *That hit the spot.*

After Devin had prepped the food, he came out to the patio. "A penny for your thoughts," he said as he approached the table.

Nanette gave a little shake of her head. "I didn't see you coming."

"Let me guess." Devin sat and poured himself a glass of red. "You were slipping back to Amanda."

She lifted her glass, took a sip, smiled big at Devin, and flared her hand out to her side. "Yes, actually, but the wine is helping."

After Devin finished his first glass of wine, he poured himself and Nanette a second. "I will get the grill going. Would you like to eat here or inside?"

"I have hardly been outside all week." She made a smiley face. "Here, please, good sir."

After dinner, which Nanette insisted on helping to clean up, they stood at the kitchen sink. Devin put his hand on Nanette's waist and leaned into her, his lips kissing her neck.

Devin could feel the heat rising in her, like a cold furnace struck with fire. She turned and looked up at him as their lips met, tongues twisting in hunger.

In her bedroom, they silently slipped out of their clothes. Devin lay on top of her; her velvety skin and sensual body only ratcheted up his desire.

As his member came inside her, Nanette lunged forward with a thrust of her hip and fell into a slow rhythm of lovemaking before the pace increased, as Devin's body and hers acted as one.

When he came with a loud grunt of pleasure, Nanette let out of a stream of air, as though a release valve had been pulled. It came over Devin that until the end of the play, moments like these might be few and far between.

After a morning session of pleasurable lovemaking, they decided on breakfast at home: oatmeal, muffins, and orange juice. By the end of the meal, Nanette had shifted back to not exactly distant, but her full attention was elsewhere, and a slight tension seemed to come over her.

Devin knew the sign and said he had chores to run, so if she needed to work on the play, no problem.

"Thank you, yes," Nanette said. "It's just that I need to iron out a few kinks in emoting various facets of Amanda's character."

And so it went, with intermittent breaks for Nanette from her rehearsals, which grew to four times a week. Mostly, they were apart.

Devin was happy for Nanette that she was so into her play, but the few times he saw her, she seemed more consumed by her character.

During one time together, when they ate Chinese on her back patio, Nanette said, "Amanda Wingfield is a complex, charmingly pitiable woman who has gotten inside me and won't let go." Her eyes grew big and her mouth opened to the wonder of it all. She was in the moment, an actress absorbed, on and off stage, by her character.

Where this left Devin, he was not sure. Maybe after the play, they would go back to what they had—two people falling in love. Now, it was Nanette falling in love all over again with the theater. After this play and her performance, which Devin knew would be stunning, would there be other plays, other opportunities?

Time will tell, he thought. *It always does.*

CHAPTER 25

THIS WAS THE DAY—NANETTE's first opening night in forty years. It had been a challenging five weeks. The rehearsals had grown to five days a week in the town library's basement. The first rehearsal included introductions of the cast and crew; then John Abbot explained the rehearsal process in detail, as well as his interpretation of the play and how the main characters react to each other. After that, the hard part began—memorizing lines before each session, developing chemistry with her fellow actors and reacting to them, practicing movement and facial expressions when listening and talking. It was an overwhelming and exhilarating time.

The dress rehearsal took place at the theater with all the crew present. Changing into different costumes between scenes was a wild free-for-all in a cramped dressing room—Nanette had to slip out of an old, faded lace dress and into an extravagant white gown, with a string of pearls that wouldn't clip on—but they pulled it off, and John's final words were, "Break a leg!"

Nanette felt like she was a part of a new family; she had thrived on the camaraderie of the rehearsal process, even inviting some fellow actors over to her house on a Saturday afternoon for hors d'oeuvres to brainstorm about the play. She had thought about asking Devin to attend but decided that he would feel out of place.

She knew she had neglected Devin, but the play—and, more precisely, Amanda Wingfield—had taken hold of Nanette. It seemed that she spent every waking moment either studying lines, rehearsing, or thinking about tweaking a delivery of a line or a reaction to a line. She dreamed about the play, dreamed that she was Amanda Wingfield, and dreamed that she was on that stage on opening night, performing with every fiber of her being.

CHAPTER 26

DEVIN PUT THE LAST TOOL away in his toolbox in the bed of his pickup, waved at another happy customer, and headed home. He had finished tiling the master bath and had installed new hardware for the sink. Usually, Devin didn't work on Saturdays, but since Nanette got involved in the theater, he preferred to keep his mind busy than stew over where he stood with her.

But one exchange between them kept clicking on in his mind, whether he was lying in bed, eating, or working. It was after they'd made love for the first time, and Devin had said, *"Promise me one thing."*

"Anything," Nanette had replied in a tone of such sincere conviction.

"You won't go on your way."

"I promise."

But it seemed she *had* gone on her way or at least had been diverted by the pull of the stage. But tonight was opening night, and Nanette had a ticket reserved for Devin at the box office. She also had asked him to join her afterward with some of the cast at Norma's.

This would be the first time they had seen each other in … three weeks? It had been a while. Over that period, Nanette had sent a couple of texts, mostly filling Devin in on the progress of rehearsals and the *interesting* people with whom she was working. There was no mention of where he and she stood. The texts seemed more like correspondence to a friend than a person with whom you were on the verge of falling in love.

Devin kept his replies straightforward, letting her know how happy he was for her—which he was—and that he couldn't wait to see her perform. He didn't mention that he feared he was losing her—or at least losing what he thought he had with her—or that acting would always come first with Nanette, and he would be second choice, if not an afterthought.

As he pulled into his driveway, Devin thought about the difficult challenges he had survived in his life: Vietnam, Gretchen, the ball-busting jobs over the years in places scattered across the country. Sometimes he had woken up in one town and thought he was living in another. Whatever happened with Nanette, he would get himself through it, so ... go to the play and the gathering afterward, see how Act II to Nanette and Devin ends, and go from there.

Devin entered the theater and took a seat in a folding chair in the third row, fourth over. People were still arriving, and there was muffled anticipation in low conversations and nervous laughter.

The theater was a converted building from its days as a library, with a stage situated at the far wall, the front curtain drawn. Calling this a theater was a stretch in Devin's mind, more like a room with a wooden stage and overhead lights, but it served its purpose. A couple of years back, he had assisted in volunteer work on repair to the stage floor, small carpentry jobs, and painting. It was a utilitarian room—seating capacity: 150 folding chairs.

He thought it weird that one of the few plays he had ever seen was *The Glass Menagerie* back in Nebraska, and here he was again. He had enjoyed it the first time, though it was a depressing story of a woman living in the past and her two grown children, on whom she kept a tight rein. It was a story about memory and nostalgia.

The rear doors to the theater were closed and the last person was seated—Devin noted a few empty seats but not many. A hush fell over the audience as the overhead lights to the theater were dimmed, and the curtain was half drawn.

After the opening commentary by the character Tom—a young man with an edgy clip to his voice that blended well with the backdrop of a dark, grim tenement wall—the other half of the curtain opened, and Devin saw Nanette seated at a table with a young woman. They were dressed in secondhand dressed that screamed late twenties/early thirties, with lace and ruffles and a simple pattern design.

The expression on Nanette's face was that of righteous impatience. She called for Tom.

Devin sat back as Nanette Brinson transformed herself into Amanda Wingfield.

CHAPTER 27

NANETTE DELIVERED HER LAST LINE, waited for the lights over her to dim, and exited the stage.

As the last scene played out, she hustled over to the cramped women's dressing quarters to change into a dress she had bought for the celebration at Norma's. Quickly changing, Nanette exhaled a deep breath. *Wow,* she thought, *I actually did it.*

She thought the play had gone well, that she and the other actors had done a fine job, but did the audience feel the same way? Did John Abbot, her exacting director, find her and the others worthy of his praise?

She looked at herself in the one mirror in the space. Her special celebratory treat was a powder blue A-line dress that was fitted to her shoulders and waist, with a modest V-neckline that exposed the top of her cleavage. She liked what she saw. She liked how she felt—complete for the first time, maybe ever.

She returned to the wings in time for the final curtain that was met by a long round of applause from the audience. *One down and one to go,* Nanette thought as she greeted her fellow actors exiting the stage. Nanette wanted to hear from John Abbot, but he was huddled in a deep conversation with his staff. No doubt they were critiquing the performance.

There was a buzz backstage as actors and crew chatted and laughed about different aspects of the play. "Right before the scene where the church bell was to ring," one of the crew members, a man in his seventies, said in an animated voice, "I thought I was going to die when the clapper fell off."

Nanette slipped out into the theater, looking for Devin. As she made her way to the rear, a few people stopped her and told her how much they enjoyed her performance. One woman said, "You were mesmerizing, my dear."

Oh, how those five words lifted Nanette. She thought she might float out of the theater, where, in the rear, she found Devin.

He wore a blue blazer, a laundered gingham shirt, creased slacks, and penny loafers. He looked stunningly handsome—his bronze face was freshly shaved, and his thicket of hair had been trimmed, parted, and combed. "You were fabulous, Nanette," Devin said as he planted a kiss on her cheek. "I mean, you gave a great performance." He cocked his head back in an appraising manner. "By the way, you look absolutely ravishing. Wow, what a dress."

"Thank you," she said softly. This was nearly too much for Nanette to comprehend. It seemed her acting skills were at a level she could not have imagined, and this hunky man in her life had stood by and waited while she pursued an old and faded dream that had come back to life. "Can we sit for a minute?" She lifted her chin toward the back row of folding chairs.

"Come on," Devin said as he took her hand. "Let us allow Ms. Garbo a moment to gather herself."

"I vant not to be *alone*," Nanette said in a thick, highbrow European accent, "but"—she smiled brightly—"a moment to be alone."

"My goodness." Devin laughed as he offered his hand for Nanette to sit. "I am in the company of a multitalented actress."

"Who knew?" Nanette said as she sat back, her eyes on the empty stage.

"I did," Devin said with meaning, "the moment I saw you on that stage."

CHAPTER 28

A COUPLE SEATED IN THE outdoor area at Norma's raised their hands and clapped softly as Devin and Nanette walked by on their way into the restaurant. "Bravo," they said in unison, showering smiles on Nanette.

"Looks like I am in the company of a celebrity," Devin said as they approached a group that was sitting and standing at the back corner of the bar.

Nanette introduced Devin to the cast and crew members, who were laughing and talking over each other in animated, excited voices. Then a man with a frizz of thinning grayish-brown hair; a sharp, angular face; and large, expressive eyes came over and wrapped his arm around Nanette. "There she is," he said through a beaming smile, "my Amanda Wingfield, who fell to me from heaven above." He raised his hands over his head in mock-preacher mode.

He reminded Devin of a proud parent.

"Devin," Nanette said, "may I introduce you to our director, John Abbot."

Devin extended his hand.

"Oh my," John said in an overly dramatic tone. "That's a firm, leathery grip you have there." He turned his attention to Nanette. "My dear, you"—he fanned his hand in front of the others—"all of you did a bang-up job."

John then began discussing inside-theater talk about adjusting the lighting during Nanette's scene where she regales about Amanda's glorious past. There was an intricate way about this man of medium build—he spoke in a rapid yet articulate voice, while an ironic, intelligent smile hovered about his lips.

"Also ..." John went on to discuss the floor spacing of the actors.

While the director talked, he had the undivided attention of his people, but Nanette listened with a squint-eyed intensity, as though absorbing each and every word. She was in her element, in her world of make believe, the actress among her peers.

After drinks at the bar, compliments of John Abbot, the group of twelve moved to a back room with a long table. More drinks and theater talk, followed by dinner and then coffee.

The evening broke up at midnight, and Devin, who had walked into town, drove Nanette home in her car. When they got to her house, he discovered she was fast asleep.

Devin opened the passenger door and lifted Nanette out of the car.

She awoke in his arms at the front door and kissed him on the cheek. "My very own Sir Galahad." Her voice was sleepy with a trace of tipsy from the three glasses of wine she had drunk over the course of the evening. "You can let me down."

Devin returned to the car for Nanette's purse and her house key.

Inside the foyer, Devin waited for Nanette's next move. He wanted to spend the night with her, to make love to her, to wake up in the morning next to her, but he could see that she was exhausted. He made a decision. "I'll let you get some rest," he said as he reached for the door.

Nanette took hold of Devin's arm. "I am going to hold you to the same promise," she said in a throaty whisper.

"Not to go on my way?"

Nanette leaned into Devin, her arm around his waist, her desirable body against his, her breath warm and inviting.

Fair enough, Devin thought as they headed to Nanette's bedroom and blissful lovemaking, after which came a deep, warm sleep.

CHAPTER 29

I T WAS THE CLOSING NIGHT of *The Glass Menagerie*, and as Nanette gave herself one final look in the dressing room mirror, she had mixed feelings. She would be glad to step back from the intensity of performing, but she would miss the camaraderie of a group of people invested in an art form, the sense of accomplishment after another strong performance, and the confidence that acting had given her, not just on stage but in her daily existence. She felt worthy.

Afterward, when there were no more rehearsals, no more shows to put on, would she sink back into that old feeling of uncertainty? John Abbot had mentioned to Nanette that he wanted her for his next play. "Not sure what, when, or where, but I assure you, my most gifted thespian, that there will be a part for you."

The ideal situation would be a break from the theater for four or five weeks to recharge her acting batteries and then begin on another play. But the Pleasantville Theater Company had nothing scheduled until next year.

Don't get ahead of yourself, she thought as she headed for the wings. She needed to concentrate on the performance at hand, to give it her very best, enjoy the closing night gathering at Norma's, and then worry about what came next.

During the performance, Nanette had complete confidence in herself on the stage and in her interaction with members of the cast as she projected the angst and hardship of a life past its prime and the pull of both painful memories and nostalgia.

After the final curtain and the exchange of congratulations with cast and crew, Nanette found Devin where she always found him after every performance, standing in the back of the theater, waiting. Since opening night and that dreamy evening together afterward, they had advanced to an understanding that they had something special between them.

Devin had been so tolerant and understanding during rehearsals when she, in looking back now, had gotten too deeply immersed in the play and the people in it. After opening night, she had entered a sensible routine of sharing time between Devin and her commitment to the show.

They saw each other after each performance—Wednesday and Saturday for four weeks—and spent Sundays together, bike riding in the park, followed by lunch on Nanette's patio. They were in a comfortable place, two people having found each other later in life.

"You had it going on tonight," Devin said as he placed a congratulatory kiss on her cheek.

"Can we sit?" Nanette asked, waving a hand toward the empty rows of folding chairs.

After they sat, Nanette said, "I felt it tonight." She squinted at Devin. "It was as though ..." She looked off for a moment and then back to Devin. "As though ..." She hesitated again and threw out a laugh.

"As though," Devin said, "the character had sunk into your bones, your being, and at that moment on stage, you were Amanda Wingfield."

Nanette clutched her arm around Devin's elbow as she realized that what he had said was so and that, also, Devin understood her like none other.

CHAPTER 30

Norma's was packed. The same spot in the corner at the bar, as on opening night, was occupied by folks involved with the play. John Abbot was regaling his listeners in full dramatic form—eyebrows raised, eyes sparkling with animation, and hand gestures with a maestro's flair to accentuate a point.

Devin only half listened during these moments of *theater talk* as he observed this collection of artists and technicians who combined their talents for a common cause. He watched the reaction of the others to the director, John Abbot, and he listened to the tone and quavers in their voices as they interacted.

Much could be learned from how people spoke to each other and how they listened. Were they rapt with attention, as Nanette had been toward Abbot at the opening-night party, or had that rapture faded into respectful listening, as she did now, as though she no longer found him the be-all-and-end-all of the theater? The crew's reaction appeared to be feigned rapt interest. He suspected they thought John Abbot a bit of a windbag.

In mid-windbag, Abbot stopped talking as a man approached the group. He was of medium size, wearing a well-tailored dark suit, and his salt-and-pepper hair that was perfectly coiffed. "James Manion!" Abbot raised his hands over his head, and his dramatic eyes flared with a look of astonishment.

"Hello, John," Manion said in a spirited hail-fellow voice.

Devin could see that this guy had an air of the charmer about him, an air of success.

"Allow me to introduce Mr. James Manion, Hollywood impresario, whom I know from my days in La-La Land."

During Abbot's introduction, Devin noticed eye contact between Nanette and Manion. It was the same type of reaction he would have had if Gretchen Winter, his first love from Manhattan Beach, had walked into the room.

Abbot asked Manion, "What brings you here, old chap?"

"I was on a scouting mission at The Villages at their fabulous theater. I'm in search of a specific character for a specific role for a film for which I am a producer." Manion slanted a knowing smile at Nanette.

"Any luck?" Abbot inquired.

Every member of the cast and crew was focused on this confident man with the Hollywood credentials.

"Not at the Sharon," Manion said as he flashed a brilliant smile at Nanette, who returned it with her own glistening beamer. "Bu-u-t-t," he said, drawing the word out with a showman's flair—eyes wide, mouth slightly agape with the wonder of it all, "I got a tip about someone in another production." He paused, as if on cue. "I believe I found what I was looking for at your very fine closing performance tonight."

"One of my actors?" Abbot said, his eyes settling on Nanette.

"Nanette," Manion said, looking directly at her, "do you remember what I told you at our forty-year reunion a few years back?"

"You know each other?" Abbot asked.

A gasp, like air releasing from a giant balloon, came from the group.

"Jimmy," Nanette said, "or, more correctly now, James and I were high school classmates."

More than just classmates, Devin thought as he felt a sinking in his gut.

"Nanette was a brilliant performer in theater way back when," Manion said. He lifted his chin to the bartender and twirled his finger, indicating another round. "I told her at our reunion that if she ever returned to performing to let me know." He turned to Nanette. "Maybe tomorrow, we could get together and discuss it further."

"I'd like that," Nanette said, as she flashed a furtive glance at Devin, as though just remembering he was present.

Nanette's promise not to go on her way now seemed in real jeopardy.

CHAPTER 31

J AMES WAS TO ARRIVE AT Nanette's house at ten in the morning, and after they discussed what he had in mind concerning a role for her, she would ask him to join her for lunch. She had gotten up early, gone to the supermarket, and just finished preparing a shrimp salad they would eat on the patio.

Nanette checked the kitchen wall clock—nine thirty. She took a seat at the nook to catch her breath. The last twenty-four hours had been a whirlwind. The excitement and rush from the last performance had barely settled in her bones when James had arrived at Norma's. A surge of old memories flooded through her at the sight of him, looking so self-confident with his place in the world. And when his eyes caught hers, she felt some knowledge pass between them, as though his eyes were saying, *Remember me? Remember us?*

She wasn't sure what to make of his offer; she still knew little about it. Last night, when she asked, James smiled and said he would rather discuss it in private.

After they had arranged the place and time, James had checked his watch and bid so long to John Abbot with a handshake. "Good seeing you, Mr. Director." He then pointed a finger at Nanette, smiling with his eyes, and said, "Until tomorrow." He then turned and left the restaurant.

Nanette thought it more than a coincidence that James had appeared last night. After Roger passed, she received flowers and a note from James with his condolences. She wasn't sure how he knew of her husband's sudden death or that she had moved to Pleasantville, although that wouldn't have been hard to find out.

Still, that didn't mean he wasn't interested in her as a performer, but she sensed that he was also interested in rekindling their relationship. And Nanette knew she wasn't the only one who thought that. She caught the deflated look in Devin's eyes as soon as James arrived. But he never brought up James, never said a word about what she was sure he had figured out—that she and James were an item back in high school. She thought of a line from the poem "Invictus" that Devin had recited:

In the fell clutch of circumstance I have not winced nor cried aloud.

In any event, she would listen to what James had to say and then take her time in making any decisions. At least, that's what she told herself.

James arrived right at ten, dressed in a short-sleeved light blue shirt with a buttoned collar and pleated cotton pants. He was holding a leather folder monogrammed with J. A. M., and Nanette remembered that his middle name was Aloysius because his friends on the tennis team teasingly had called him that.

They sat at the kitchen nook, where James opened his folder and removed a thick stack of eight-and-a-half-by-eleven, three-hole-punched white papers, secured by round-head fasteners. The top sheet had a title in courier-style font that Nanette could not make out, below which was what she thought was a name.

"Is that the script for the film you want to discuss?" Nanette inquired.

"Have you heard of Mason Reynolds?"

"Yes," Nanette said. "He won the Pulitzer for fiction a few years back for *A Childless Mother*—I haven't gotten around to reading it yet."

"Well, then," James said as he tapped the script with his index finger, "this is the adapted screenplay." He lifted his brow, his eyes saying, *Interested?* James went on to give a brief summary of the story of a single mother and her relationship with her twenty-year-old daughter, who had joined a religious cult in Utah and would have no contact with her mother.

"What is the role you have in mind for me?" Nanette asked.

"Julia, the mother," James said with a nod.

"How old is Julia?"

"Midforties."

"I'm too—"

"Nanette," James said, "you do not look your age." He lifted a finger. "And we have an excellent makeup department."

"So, are you offering me the part, or do I have to audition?"

"You would audition," James said. He folded his hands on the table and leaned forward, his eyes drawing in Nanette. "But I will have a big say, and I am also confident that after the rest of the power brokers see you and see your audition"—he drew in a breath and sat back, his lips parting in a knowing smile—"they will want you as badly as I do." James cringed, the corner of his mouth twisting downward. "I should rephrase that. Want you for the *part* as badly as I do."

"If I agree to the audition," Nanette said cautiously, "where would it take place—and when?"

"We've rented an audition space at the Beverly Hills Hotel."

"Wow."

"Have you been there?" James asked with lifted brow.

"Years ago, my husband took me on a business trip to Beverly Hills, and we had lunch in the Polo Lounge," Nanette said as the memory ran through her mind. It was the most luxurious hotel she had ever been in; it included private bungalows, lush fragrant gardens, and public areas reminiscent of timeless Hollywood glamour. Nanette had loved everything about the place, and she remembered thinking that if she had continued acting and had found success, she might have been a guest there often.

"Nanette," James said, "you must audition, or I fear you will regret not having done so for the rest of your life."

Nanette said nothing for a moment; her eyes were on James, who had a look that said, *Come on; give it a shot.*

"When do I audition?"

CHAPTER 32

O N SUNDAY MORNING, DEVIN ROSE from his own bed for the first Sunday since *The Glass Menagerie* had opened. Last night at Norma's, Nanette had begged off, citing her meeting with Manion in the morning.

Manion seemed like a nice enough guy, though Devin thought he had an interest in more than Nanette's acting. When Manion had first arrived last night, and he and Nanette had exchanged looks, there was a naked, raw longing in his eyes for a moment before he caught himself and returned to the role of magnanimous Hollywood big shot.

And Nanette's eyes also had a spark of interest in this old flame from her high school days, as she listened intently while Manion spoke. At that exact moment, Devin had felt a separation come between them, an invisible yet palatable cold front that had neutered that charge of interest between them.

Another change to his Sunday routine would be to take a bike ride alone. Devin retrieved his bike from the bike rack out back and walked it out to the street. He decided to take the long way around to the park and avoid Nanette's house, where Manion would be trying to sell her on some role in a movie.

Devin couldn't see Nanette turning down the opportunity to perform in a Hollywood production. If she asked for his advice, Devin would tell her that if she liked the part, she should take it. He just hoped this wasn't some ruse on Manion's part to spark a romance with Nanette. That she had little or no chance, and he desired to have his way with her and check off another notch on his bucket list.

He decided to take two runs around Seminole Park—thirty miles in all. He wanted to ride hard and let the physical exertion ease his body, as well as ease his mind from the thought that his relationship with Nanette had entered another unknown zone with myriad options. She could turn down the offer flat and send Manion on his way—doubtful, very doubtful; she could audition, not get the part, and return home unscathed from any romance with Manion; she could—*Stop it,* Devin told himself, as he could run these scenarios through his mind endlessly.

The loop at Seminole Park had too many bikers and pedestrians for Devin's liking, so he locked the bike to a post at a picnic shelter and walked into the park's interior on a dirt trail. It was a warm day—the temperature was expected to reach over ninety—but the canopy of trees provided good shade.

The dirt trail was wide enough for two, and as he meandered along a creek, he thought how much Nanette would have enjoyed its soothing gurgle, complemented by the bustle and chirps of birds rustling in the tall trees and in the thicket of shrubs and wildflowers. Devin walked at a steady clip along the creek, where the belch of a bullfrog now joined the chorus of chirping birds—he imagined how Nanette would have reacted, her face aglow at the wonder of it all.

When he emerged from the interior, he came to a spot on the lake where he and Nanette had witnessed a great blue heron standing perfectly still—it had grasped an enormous fish from the water in its long pointed beak and swallowed it whole. They had seen beaver swimming across the lake and alligators basking in the sun.

Those moments together—as she watched in awe and appreciation and then flashed her winning smile at Devin, as if to say thank you for this—brought out a sigh in him.

Would they ever share another time here together—just the two of them, appreciating the scene before them and each other's company?

After a two-hour walkabout and building up a good sweat, Devin decided to ride past Nanette's house on the way back. As he approached, he saw a black BMW parked in Nanette's driveway behind her car. He slowed as he rode by, not sure what he was looking for.

Once past Nanette's house, Devin had an intuition. The house next to Nanette's was for sale and vacant. He couldn't believe he was doing this, but he went to the far side of the empty house and peered around the corner toward Nanette's backyard, where he saw her and

Manion eating on the patio. They appeared to be having a fine time. Manion said something, and Nanette leaned back in a full laugh. Devin imagined Manion was recalling some incident from their high school past.

On the table was the same serving bowl in which Nanette had served Devin shrimp salad. Was she also serving that delectable meal to Manion—of all people? A sudden, empty, gut-wrenching feeling came over Devin, a feeling he had not experienced since Gretchen Winter had left him in Manhattan Beach all those years ago.

CHAPTER 33

"**T**HAT'S THE BEST SHRIMP SALAD I have ever eaten," James said as he eased back in his chair, patting his stomach.

"Thank you," Nanette said. It passed in her mind that Devin had made the same comment.

"Well," James said in a tone that indicated the next order of business. "I best get going. I have a plane to catch." Nanette walked James to the door. James turned in the foyer and faced her. "I will email you the airline ticket to LAX, where a driver will be waiting at the airport to take you to the hotel."

"I can't believe this is happening," Nanette said.

James put his hand on Nanette's shoulder, his eyes fixed on hers. "Two weeks, Nanette; I will see you in Los Angeles."

Nanette thought he might try to kiss her, so she extended her hand, which James grasped and shook. His hand was small and soft in comparison to Devin's. "Safe trip, James," Nanette said with hand raised.

After James left, Nanette's phone rang. "Hello, Connor," she said in a hurried voice on her way to the kitchen.

"How did closing night go?"

Nanette had kept her son up-to-date on her rediscovered acting career but had not mentioned Devin. "It went great." She heard a tremor in her voice. She did not want to mention James or her trip to Hollywood.

"Everything OK?" Connor asked. "You sound a bit flustered."

"I'm still trying to unwind from the play—it was a lot of work," she said as she eased into a seat at the kitchen nook.

"Ah," Connor said, seeming unconvinced. He went on to say that he was departing on a month-long research cruise the next day and that communicating would be difficult. After he gave some details about his cruise, which was to focus on estimating the abundance of middle-depth fish species in subarctic areas, and after Nanette small-talked about life in Florida and returning to the stage—"It was an exhilarating experience"— Connor said he had errands to run to prepare for his cruise.

"Have a great time," Nanette said, feeling a sense of relief that she wouldn't have to omit parts of her life to her son for the next few weeks. "And don't worry about your mother; I'm doing fine."

After hanging up, Nanette exhaled deeply. She didn't like holding things back from Connor, but she wasn't sure how he would react to Devin and especially her taking off for Los Angeles, where James would be waiting, someone who had returned to her life before she had a husband and son. The next time they talked, things possibly might be clearer.

She went to the patio, put the empty plates on a tray, and returned to the kitchen. When she had served Devin this meal, he had helped with the cleanup. It came to her that Devin might feel excluded, possibly shunned, by what had transpired over the last twenty-four hours, especially her canceling his spending Saturday night and their Sunday bike ride.

She picked up her cell phone and called Devin.

"Hello, Ms. Garbo," Devin said.

It felt good to hear his voice, still with his good humor. "I thought I'd fill you in on what happened with my meeting with James."

"Let me guess," Devin said. "You are going to Los Angeles for a screen test."

"And I will be staying at the Beverly Hills Hotel." Nanette laughed. "Can you believe it?"

"I'm really happy for you," Devin said. In a more serious tone, he asked, "What's the part?"

"James gave me the script for my audition for *A Childless Mother*."

"I've read the book—great story," Devin said. "I'm guessing you will be playing the mother. What was her name? Ah yes, Julia." There was silence on the line before Devin said, "When are you leaving?"

"Two weeks," Nanette said, as the weight of her decision hit her. She felt suddenly vulnerable, suddenly in need of Devin's company. "I know this is last-minute, but would you like to come over and maybe order carryout for dinner?"

"How about I ride my bike over, and we take our morning bike ride in the afternoon?"

"Yes," Nanette said with meaning. "I would like that."

CHAPTER 34

WHEN DEVIN HAD SEEN NANETTE'S name pop up on his phone's screen, a surge of hope had filled him. Since seeing Manion on Nanette's back patio, Devin hadn't done anything other than sitting on his back deck, staring off into space. But her call spurred him to take a quick shower and get himself over to her place.

He needed to quit jumping to conclusions in regard to him and Nanette. He tried to tell himself not to get too high and not get too low. But it was hard because Nanette Brinson had captured his heart. That was the truth and there was no way around it. Had he captured her heart? At times, he thought he possibly had, but it seemed to fluctuate with what was going on in her life.

He figured that she had called him after the meeting with Manion because, yes, she wanted to see him, to be with him. More than that, though, going to Hollywood for an audition was a big deal, a possibly life-altering deal, and good old Devin was her stable rock to lean on.

As Devin got out of the shower, he told himself not to overthink it and to enjoy her company.

The traffic had eased up at the park, but the heat and humidity had ratcheted up since that morning. They rode at a slow, easy pace, stopping a couple of times along the way to take in the views. During those breaks Nanette was pensive, her mind seemingly on other matters, as Devin pointed to a beaver leaving a small wake as he swam across the lake before submerging.

"Oh," Nanette said in a half-hearted tone.

"You'll do just fine," Devin said.

Nanette winced. "It's just that," she said haltingly. "I don't know if I want to …" Her voice trailed off as she turned to Devin, her eyes vulnerable and uncertain.

"If you don't take this audition, will you regret it down the road?"

"That's what James said to me," Nanette said with a slight smile.

"Why not take the audition?" Devin said. He pointed to the beaver emerging from the water with the thick root of an aquatic plant. "And go from there." He didn't want to say that she might not get the part and that would be the end of it or that Manion might have ulterior motives.

They watched the beaver make a beeline for the shore, where he stopped in a shallow and began chomping down his catch.

"Yes," Nanette said, "I must see it through." A smile flickered at the corner of her mouth. "And if I don't get the part, I can always say I tried."

"You are a talented actress, Nanette," Devin said as he watched the beaver leave the shallows and disappear into the cover of the woods. "You know that." He gave Nanette a knowing lift of his brow. "So my advice"—he hesitated and looked at Nanette, who nodded for him to continue—"is to look upon it as an adventure—the stay at the Beverly Hills Hotel, the interesting people you will meet, the chance to show Hollywood your plentiful talent."

"That's it, an adventure." There was renewed excitement in her voice.

Devin hoped he wouldn't regret his words. She might find huge success in Hollywood, move to Southern California, and leave Devin back at square one—alone, just him and his handyman tools.

CHAPTER 35

NANETTE HADN'T NOTICED THAT HER seat was in first class until she checked in at the airport. As she nestled into the window seat, a flight attendant handed her a menu, which included a list of complimentary drinks. "Thank you," Nanette said. She sank into the comfort of the roomy leather and stretched her legs out with ample room. *I could get used to this*, she thought.

As the plane taxied down the runway, Nanette gripped the armrest. She was in a two-seat row; the other seat was empty. Takeoffs had always made her a bit nervous, and she would always clutch Roger's hand until the plane reached its set altitude. But to her surprise, her stomach stayed calm with the whistling roar of the plane hurtling down the runway, the hydraulic groan of the landing gears retracting, and the plane shaking when it hit turbulence.

When the plane reached cruising altitude, the seatbelt sign came off, and she clicked her seat back a notch. She felt good—a calm good. Why the takeoff had not rattled her, she did not know. Maybe her new life paradigm had altered more than she had suspected. Perhaps no longer being dependent on Roger and having Devin in her life had something to do with it.

The last couple of weeks with Devin had been grand. With his help, she had practiced the scene for which she would audition. Devin had read the lines of the daughter of Nanette's character, Julia. He even offered advice on reacting to a line: "Show a bit more apprehension in your eyes." He also mentioned she should take her time when delivering her lines. "I reread the book, and Julia is cautious and careful when speaking with her only child."

Once Nanette had the lines down and felt as comfortable as Julia as she had as Amanda in *The Glass Menagerie*, a confidence came over her—she could handle this role.

In the times between concentrating on the scene, Devin and Nanette had been so comfortable together, whether on a Sunday bike ride or teaming up to cook out in her backyard. Nanette would buy the food and prepare the side dishes, and Devin would cook whatever the main course was on the grill. They would sit on her back patio—a glass of wine for her, a bottle of beer for Devin—and relax in the comfort of each other's company. Nanette's only regret about leaving now wasn't a fear of the audition but in leaving Devin for the next week.

James had booked her at the Beverly Hills Hotel for Sunday through Saturday. "There may be multiple auditions," he had told Nanette, "so in between, you can enjoy the hotel, and maybe I can take you to my favorite place on Rodeo Drive."

Rodeo Drive was the most luxurious street Nanette had ever been on. When she and Roger visited Beverly Hills, she strolled down Rodeo Drive by herself, and it was a thrill. She'd had lunch at a deli and had seen Mel Brooks standing in line, throwing rapid-fire lines at a young beauty, who held her pose and smiled, as if experiencing a common occurrence.

Nanette had gone up and down both sides of this otherworldly street, window-shopping at the haute boutiques and watching the glamorous women, young and old, in their expensive clothes, lavish diamond bracelets and necklaces, and gold watches.

One memory that stayed vivid was the superior air of many of the people on Rodeo Drive, as though they were walking this street modeling their lofty attainments in this life.

The entire experience of Rodeo Drive had shocked and mesmerized Nanette. The over-the-top opulence had repulsed but at the same time attracted her. She remembered thinking that if she ever became a movie actress and attained a level of success, she would never allow herself to act in such a manner. But could such a modus operandi subconsciously but relentlessly alter one's persona with stealthy efficacy? And if, by chance, that was recognized later in life, would it be too late after so many years, because you were no longer that person and saw your life through a different prism?

The plane landed on time at three thirty, and after retrieving her luggage at the baggage area, Nanette saw a man in a dark suit, holding a sign with her name on it.

"Hello," Nanette said.

"Ms. Brinson," the man said as he reached for her bag. "Allow me."

Here I go, Nanette thought as she followed her chauffeur out of the terminal and to an awaiting enormous black SUV.

When her ride turned off Sunset Boulevard and into the entrance to the hotel, it all came back to Nanette—the driveway lined by palm trees and tropical flora. She craned forward to take in the white palatial mission adorned with turrets and domes that sat on a hill, with verandas and arches and a peachy-pink porte cochere, dusted with gold, green, and white-striped accents, where a red carpet awaited.

A bellhop in a black vest, white shirt, gloves, and a lime-green tie approached the vehicle. He opened the back door and said, "Ms. Brinson, I presume." He then smiled as though approving of the lady before him.

Nanette had bought a mauve blouse with a matching lace scarf, cotton-knit white skirt, and black leather pumps with one-inch heels for the trip—casual chic was what Devin had called it.

"Yes," Nanette said, a bit startled and also a bit thrilled at the attention.

"Mr. Manion requested I take you to your bungalow." The chauffeur had removed Nanette's luggage from the rear, and the bellhop placed it on a luggage cart. "If you would follow me, ma'am."

Off Nanette went onto the red carpet and into the lobby, past the check-in desk, following the bellhop down a corridor. She had to remind herself this was really happening, that she was a guest not only at this most exclusive of hotels but that James had gotten her a private bungalow. It was a bit disconcerting to think he was going to all this expense for an unknown actress's audition.

Inside bungalow number five, Nanette thanked the bellhop and took ten dollars out of her purse and handed it to him. "Thank you," she said. She hoped it was enough. She hadn't thought about tipping.

The bellhop thanked her and handed her an envelope. "From Mr. Manion," he said.

She placed the note on a side table and took a look-see of her residence for the next week. She stood in a spacious sitting area with big, comfortable-looking armchairs and a primping table and mirror, beyond which she entered a bedroom with a king-sized bed and French doors that she opened to discover a swimming pool. "Oh my," Nanette said aloud as she stepped out onto the pool deck.

Back in the sitting area, she opened the note. "James here. Welcome Nanette. I will be tied up until late tonight but have the audition scheduled for ten tomorrow morning in the Rodeo Ballroom—see you then!"

Nanette suddenly felt far away, although from what she was not sure. She reached for her cell phone and called Devin.

CHAPTER 36

DEVIN WAS SITTING ON HIS back deck, watching the sun sink below the horizon. It had been a long, strange day. He had spent the night with Nanette, arising on Sunday morning to get her to Orlando International Airport in her car, which he had volunteered to drive instead of his pickup, and which she quickly had accepted.

After checking her luggage at the redcap station and sharing a farewell hug and kiss, Devin watched Nanette walk toward the terminal, stop at the entrance, and turn. She lifted her hand to Devin; a *here-goes* smile beamed at him. Nanette's smile was a special thing, with bright things in it, but beneath the outward beauty, a complex of guises were beginning to emerge. Devin thought Nanette had lived in a shell as a mother and wife, doing her duties while submerging her talent. And now that she was no longer suppressed, all sorts of different facets of her personality were emerging, as though an internal battle was occurring over who would emerge.

The ring of his cell phone broke his train of thought. "Have they measured your handprint for the Hollywood Walk of Fame yet?" Devin said into the receiver.

Nanette laughed and then described the hotel and her private bungalow. "It's overwhelming," she said.

"Have you gotten a schedule yet for the audition?"

"Tomorrow at ten—with probably more."

"Ah, yes," Devin said, "the unknown. Life's way of keeping you on your toes."

"I'll call you tomorrow after the audition," Nanette said.

"Nanette?" Devin said, a change in his voice.

"Yes."

"You will knock their socks off. I can already see it." Silence. "Are you there?"

"That's what scares me," Nanette replied.

"Maybe now, but afterward, you will adjust and be glad for it." Again, Devin hoped his words didn't lead to his demise with regard to this woman he loved.

"I'm glad I have you, Devin."

"And me, you."

"I'll call tomorrow," Nanette said.

Devin wanted to say *I love you* but instead said, "I'll be here."

CHAPTER 37

NANETTE ARRIVED AT THE AUDITION and found James huddled in a far corner with a young man and young woman—assistants, she assumed. The Rodeo Ballroom was a large, open space with a black piano on a stage in front of drawn curtains and a round table with high-back chairs in the middle of the room, where James was heading. The space looked perfect for a wedding.

"Nanette," James said with gleeful vigor. He waved her over to the table and made introductions to Annie, his personal assistant, and Jeremy, an assistant casting director.

"We have a bit of a delay," James said. His two fellow producers were running late. "Hollywood time is not normal time." He made a face, as though an idea had come to him. "Have a seat," he said, indicating the last empty chair. "Would you like a coffee?"

Nanette anxiously waited for over an hour, while James took one call after another with high-pitched energy. "Alex, how is my most favorite agent?" or "Tonya, darling, me oh my, how good it is to hear your voice."

Finally, two men in their fifties appeared, both dressed in tennis shorts and short-sleeved, cotton-knit white shirts with upturned collars. They looked like Hollywood fat cats or over-aged frat boys after a day of fun in the sun.

Jeremy and Annie, as though on cue, got up from their seats, which the fat cats settled in, bringing with them an air of detached distraction, as though a shadow had been cast over the room.

After James introduced Reggie and Barry, he told Nanette that Annie would read the daughter's part.

"Can we do it on the stage?" Nanette asked.

"But of course," James said as he offered his hand toward the stage.

On stage, Annie began reading her script: "You never really loved me. You were a fake mother in your fake world."

"Darling," Nanette said ever so carefully, as it came to her that this was her moment, this was her time, and she should let it all out.

At the end of the audition, Nanette looked at the table. James had a broad smile of approval. Barry and Reggie were nodding, as if to say, *Not bad, not bad at all.*

As Nanette stepped off the stage, James approached. "We have a few more auditions," he said with a glance at a woman standing off near the entrance. She was dressed in tight-fitting slacks and a V-neck short-sleeved blouse, and she possessed a certain mature look of dramatic flair—her eyes wide and alert, her auburn hair in a midlength breezy do, and her body fit and curvy. "May I take you to dinner tonight?"

Nanette slid another look at the woman in the wings; she recognized her now as Sandra Sommers, a star in her twenties. Over the years, her career had faded, as often was the case with women, as Nanette hadn't seen her on the big screen for a good while.

"Nanette?" James said with a hint of impatience. "Dinner?"

"Yes, James, that would be nice."

Nanette decided to eat lunch at the hotel's outdoor dining area, the Polo Terrace off the Polo Lounge. The space had a Mexican flair, with a pink-tiled scalloped roof and matching arches. It brought to mind a garden with trees and flowers and trellised vines. She was escorted to a table for two under a gnarled tree that her server informed her was a Brazilian pepper tree.

How exotic, Nanette thought as she took in the scene before her. The patrons were talking in low voices; she surmised that some were tourists by their wide-eyed expressions, as though they had arrived in the promised land. Others had more of a been-there/done-that look, though with a manner of appreciation for the life they were living.

After lunch, Nanette returned to her room and contemplated the day's events. She could tell that James was pleased with her performance, but Barry and Reggie, she was not sure. And Sandra Sommers, in the wings, might be one of the other producers' picks, possibly even a romantic interest.

She thought about calling Devin but told herself to wait until she knew more. Why bother calling him with no news? Also, she didn't want to tell him about going out to dinner with James that night and have him worry unnecessarily.

She decided to stroll about the grounds of the hotel. She changed into Bermuda shorts she had purchased for the trip, a blouse-shirt with buttons from neck to below her chest, and comfy canvas walking shoes.

The walk around the property was fascinating—so many nooks and cocoon-like spaces, the beautiful lawn garden with an array of plants and trees.

Back in her bungalow, Nanette changed into her one-piece bathing suit and flip-flops. She studied herself in the bathroom mirror. There was still shape to her body—her breasts with form and depth, her arms with a firmness, and the skin under her neck smooth and supple. Still, she was a sixty-year-old woman with thin wrinkles crinkling out at the corner of each eye, an incursion that grew a little more prominent with each passing year.

She liked to tell herself that she wasn't worried about her looks, but deep down, she knew it was a lie. Of course, she cared about how she looked, especially now at the Beverly Hills Hotel, for heaven's sake.

She put on a T-shirt over her bathing suit, grabbed a romance novel she had purchased at the Orlando airport, and stepped out onto the bungalow pool deck, where the only other person sitting poolside was someone she had seen earlier that day—Sandra Sommers.

Nanette sat in a patio chair at a table with the umbrella up, across the pool from her competition. Sandra was stretched out in a lounge chair, scrolling through a script. She was wearing a skimpy bikini that highlighted her lean, shapely body. She glanced across the pool in Nanette's direction through a large pair of tortoiseshell sunglasses— she looked every bit the Hollywood actress, and Nanette felt like an interloping tourist poaching her territory.

Nanette could not tell if Sandra was looking at her directly, but Sandra made no acknowledgement of her presence as she returned her attention to her script. There was an aloofness to this woman, an

Dennis McKay

insouciant air of—Nanette remembered the famous Greta Garbo line: *I vant to be alone.*

Oh yes, Nanette thought as a swell of guilt came on her. She needed to at least let Devin know she was OK. She decided to text him. "Audition went well. Call you when know more."

CHAPTER 38

LATE AFTERNOON ON MONDAY, DEVIN was applying a light broom finish to a ten-by-ten concrete slab he had poured for a shed. He had arrived at eight, set his string lines on stakes, and dug out the earth, which he loaded on his truck next to the project. He had then formed the slab, graded for four-inch depth, and laid down wire mesh.

When he finished, the concrete truck arrived right on time, and he wheeled the concrete from the driveway to the backyard, screeded, bull-floated, and troweled the slab—a one-man finishing crew.

The intensity of the work at hand had taken his mind off Nanette's audition, for the most part, but by the time he finished, it was four o'clock, and her audition had been three hours earlier. He was tempted to call her but held up; she'd said she would call. Maybe the audition was running late. Maybe she was in a meeting of some sort—who knew? It was Hollywood, after all.

By the time Devin got home, it was nearly six. He grabbed a beer from the refrigerator, went out on his back deck, and sat in an Adirondack chair. He felt the labor of the day. His shoulders were stiff from wheeling the concrete, and his body had a general weariness from the day's hard work. Usually, he had a sense of accomplishment after a good day of labor; he'd sit back, sip on a cold beer, and let his mind and body unwind. But there was no unwinding; instead, there was a tightening in his gut as it became clear that Nanette should have called him by now. She knew he would be wondering and possibly worrying, so why not call?

Then his phone chimed, indicating a new message. He texted back the thumbs-up emoji.

He was relieved that Nanette had contacted him but also hurt that she didn't bother to call. Something was up, though Devin could only speculate what it might be—but he would bet that James Manion had something to do with it.

Devin got another beer from the fridge and sat back in the Adirondack. This deck was his sanctuary that he had built with his own two hands. Of all the different structures he had constructed, this was the one he had gotten the most out of. He'd sit back with a cold beer in hand and take in his neatly trimmed yard and the foliage he had planted—the spiny agave plants bordering the deck, the areca palms along the back fence, the thick carpet of Bermuda grass that he weeded on a continual basis.

Kicking back on this deck usually had a relaxing effect on Devin. He knew he needed to stop fretting and let things come as they may. But as he had told himself before, it was easier said than done. What if she won the role and stayed in California? Then what? He had to at least brace himself for the chance that he might lose her. And if that did occur, would he, like the poet said, "Remain captain of my soul"?

CHAPTER 39

For her dinner with James, Nanette picked out a pencil skirt, a button-down top with three-quarter-length sleeves—she did not want to wear anything suggestive—and one-inch heels. She sat at the vanity table in the sitting area, applying mascara. She hadn't used mascara since she began dating Devin, but she was at the Beverly Hills Hotel in Beverly Hills, California, so why not? And while she was at it, why not dab a touch of the French perfume she had purchased at the gift shop, on a whim, on her wrists and neck? This was a once-in-a-lifetime experience, after all.

Nanette knew that famous actresses had stayed in these bungalows; Marilyn Monroe and Elizabeth Taylor were often guests. One of them might have stayed in this room she was in now. Oh, the stories these walls could tell.

After a final look in the mirror, Nanette nodded her approval—the mascara, a burgundy-wine shade, highlighted her eyelashes and sparkling eyes, which burst with life. She looked different, not so much her features that the makeup had highlighted, but there was a textured glow, as though saying, *Hello, world!*

She had told James she would meet him in the lobby, not wanting him to come to her room. It wasn't that she didn't trust him or herself, but she wanted to make clear her parameters.

Her mind flashed back to her senior year of high school, when James had transferred from California and immediately had fallen in with the in-crowd, of which Nanette was a part.

Even back then, Jimmy Manion had a way of easing himself into a group or, as in her case, becoming a romantic interest. But it wasn't until early spring that they got together. Jimmy had been dating a cheerleader until he broke up with her. Rumor around school was that she was too bossy. But that was just a rumor.

At a patio party of a girlfriend of Nanette, Jimmy asked her to dance. "My favorite song," he said to a sitting Nanette. He offered his hand. "Would the pretty girl do me the honor?"

The song was *Louie, Louie* by the Kingsmen, which Jimmy later said told the story of a wayward Jamaican sailor returning to the island to see his lover. Jimmy was the finest, smoothest dancer Nanette had ever shared a dance floor with. He moved with a confident, coordinated ease as he took her hand and twirled her under their arms, then rolled his arm off her arm, and then did the double-arm twirl.

By the end of the night, Nanette had herself a new boyfriend, a young guy committed to the social life. There wasn't a party he didn't want to attend or a gathering of friends he didn't join, and if there was social interaction among the in-crowd, Jimmy Manion was there.

She thought about the night she almost went all the way with Jimmy at the drive-in movie. They were in the back seat of his family's station wagon. Nanette was in a skirt and blouse that Jimmy had his hand up. She had promised to save herself for marriage, but at that moment, she wavered, as a fever of desire descended on her. Jimmy whispered in Nanette's ear as he eased his hand up her thigh. "I have protection."

"OK," Nanette gasped.

Jimmy leaned back from her and into a sitting position. He removed a condom from his pocket, struggled to open it, and finally secured it on.

That momentary pause brought Nanette back to earth. "No," she said in a firm voice, as Jimmy came back down on top of her with his pants and underwear down to his ankles.

He continued forward, and she felt his stiff member, wrapped in rubber, graze her upper thigh. For a moment, Nanette thought he might force himself on her.

"Goddamn it!" Nanette shouted with all the power she could muster. "I. Said. No." Never in her life had Nanette been so forceful.

Jimmy relented.

After graduation, Jimmy's family moved back to California. "My mother misses her SoCal sunshine and the laid-back life," Jimmy told

Nanette. She and Jimmy didn't actually break up but rather took new directions in their lives. They wrote to each other for the first half of their freshmen year of college, but that soon tapered off. Nanette began dating at her school, and she assumed Jimmy had done the same.

In a way, their reunion was like a movie about an unfulfilled romance, a to-be-continued serial in which the couple had been apart for forty years.

Nanette wondered what would have happened if James hadn't left for California and had stayed on the East Coast. Would they have stayed together and married? How different would her life have been? Would James have encouraged her to pursue her acting career? She thought so, but as she had learned with Roger, marriage can change the dynamics of a relationship.

But James had convinced her now to pursue a role in a major film. The thought struck her—what if she did win the role? Then what? She would be on location for a couple of months, she assumed. Would she be asked to move to Los Angeles? She could imagine James saying, "Hollywood is where you need to be if you want a real career, not some small town in the middle of Florida."

And last, where would that leave her and Devin? She was torn between her renewed passion for acting and a good man, the likes of which she had never known—a man whose company she enjoyed immensely, a man who made her feel complete.

She pushed back her chair and stood. "Don't get ahead of yourself," she said to her reflection. If she won the role—a big *if*—she then would decide.

Nanette arrived a few minutes early and waited in a sitting area of the lobby. She sat in a comfortable leather chair that was part of a circle of similar chairs around the perimeter of a beautiful floral-motif green carpet; in the middle of the carpet were vases holding white carnations atop a glass table. People were coming and going, mostly dressed in upscale casual wear—men in polo shirts and shorts or slacks and women in silk dresses and knitted blouses, with a few in shorts. There was a magical aura about this hotel of arches, verandas, and flowers everywhere—such a lovely place.

At seven, James arrived, wearing a cashmere V-neck sweater with a white dress shirt—no tie—slacks, and penny loafers. He looked very LA smooth. "Nanette," he said with a tilt of his head, eyes aslant, and a devilish smile splitting his lips. "You look fab-u-lous."

"That's what you used to say to me every time you came by for a date," Nanette said as she stood.

"I meant it then, and I mean it now," James said. He offered Nanette his elbow, which she took, and escorted her out of the hotel.

Le Connoisseur was located on Rodeo Drive in the heart of Beverly Hills. They sat in the outdoor dining area off the sidewalk, which reminded Nanette of Norma's back in Pleasantville, which seemed so far, far away.

"This is my favorite spot that I mentioned to you," James said. His attention was diverted as a man in a Hawaiian shirt with a huge gold chain around his neck came up to the table. He tapped his fist on the table, shot James a shit-eating grin, and went on his way.

And so the evening went—drinks were ordered, and people stopped by to say a brief hello to James, who seemed to know everyone. Nanette was anxious to find out what her status was regarding the audition, but she didn't want to press it. She decided to let the evening unfold as her second and then third white wine came and went. She didn't feel drunk but comfortably tipsy.

James recommended the shrimp cocktail for an appetizer and then the halibut. "That is out of this world."

Nanette was enjoying everything about the evening—the ambience of the cozy space under a string of soft lights hanging from the overhead awning, James's easy-as-you-go company. And to think that a year ago, she was a lonely, neglected housewife in a life absent of dreams.

James was right; the appetizer and main course were delicious. Over the course of the meal, James brought up the audition. "I thought your performance was excellent," he said as he lifted a hand in goodbye to a couple with whom he had exchanged hellos earlier.

"But?" Nanette said.

"One of my partners has his own favorite choice."

"Sandra Sommers?" Nanette said, with a lift of an inquiring brow.

"You saw her at the audition, I take it."

"She's rather famous—or was," Nanette said. She sat back as the waiter came to clear the table.

The waiter asked if there was anything else, and James looked at Nanette.

"I'll take a decaf tea, please." She wanted to settle down, as the wine inside her, like a friendly flame, had brought out a yearning of a grand old memory of her and James, way back when. The best-looking couple in the class of '68 was what their friends had called them.

"Make that two," James said to the waiter. He turned his attention back to Nanette. "Yes, it's a common story in this make-believe land—fame can be rather fleeting." He took a sip of water, placed his elbows on the table, and folded his hands under his chin. "This is a big opportunity for Sandra Sommers to revive her career." He unfolded his hands and splayed them out. "A big opportunity for you to begin a career—the unknown talent who returns to her first love after forty years. Hollywood loves a story like yours." James opened his eyes wide, just like he had done in high school, a boyish expression of wonder. "You're scheduled for another audition Wednesday morning at eleven—same place." He made a face that asked, *How do you like that?*

The waiter arrived with their tea on a tray, along with a cruet of honey, creamer, and sugar.

Nanette added some honey to her tea, stirred, and took a sip. She looked over at James, who had a bemused, knowing grin plastered on his face. "What?" she said.

"When I said unknown talent who returns to her *first love*"—he added cream to his tea, took a careful sip, and threw a look at Nanette—"I meant that as a double entendre." James reached across the table and took Nanette's hand, his touch warm and inviting. "You are the one I let get away—*my* first love."

On the way back to the hotel, James suggested an after-dinner drink at the Polo Lounge. Nanette hesitated momentarily before agreeing. *What the heck?* she thought, as she was still feeling the effects of three glasses of wine. If she was going to let the evening unfold, then *let the evening unfold.*

The thought flashed in her head—about success subconsciously altering one's persona—before it skipped off and away. She revisited

James's comment about her being his first love, which had not surprised her all that much. She'd known it when she first saw him back in Pleasantville by the dreamy look in his eyes when he looked at her.

But to hear him say it had caused her mind to wonder—what would it be like to be involved with a Hollywood honcho, to begin a new life as a professional actress in Hollywood with the backing of someone with the clout of James Manion?

They sat in high-back chairs at the ebonized oak bar. Nanette looked up. "Oh," she said, "I hadn't noticed the candy-striped ceiling."

"I think it goes well with the rich green walls," James said as he lifted his finger to the bartender.

Nanette requested a Chablis, and James, a stinger.

James lifted his chin to a photo behind the bar of two men playing polo. "You know who they are?" he asked.

"I recognize Will Rogers," Nanette said.

Their drinks were served; James's stinger was accompanied by a gardenia. "Now that's an old-time Hollywood drink." He lifted the flower, and placed it on the bar, and took a sip of his drink, followed by a satisfying *ah*. "The other gentleman," he said, returning his attention to the photograph, "is Darryl F. Zanuck, a big-time Hollywood legend, who did it his way."

Nanette swiveled her stool around, smiled at James, and took in the space before her. The bar had an appealing design—table lamps and the ever-present flowers, dark-green booths—and on the other side of a glass wall, the Polo Lounge was aglitter in soft light. There was a trapped-in-amber feeling that had a comforting effect of being in an otherworldly cocoon. "And," Nanette said in a teasing tone, "is James Manion doing it his way?"

"Yes," James said in a straightforward manner. "And is Nanette Brinson on the brink of doing it *her* way?"

"I guess," Nanette said as she lifted her wine. "That is my sixty-four-thousand-dollar question." She took a swallow of her drink and looked off momentarily, then back at James. She leaned forward, clasped his neck, and kissed him on the cheek. "Thank you"—she opened her hand, palm up, and swept it out to her side—"for all this." She took another swallow of wine, and it passed briefly through her mind that she was more than a little tipsy.

Nanette woke with a start, her head pounding; the wine from the previous night was having its way with her. She peeled back the covers and found that she was naked—buck naked! Bits and pieces from the night swirled in her mind.

James had come back to her room, where more wine was drunk, and then—*Oh, my God*. She and James had engaged in a night of sexual romps. Three times, if she remembered correctly: James on top, then Nanette on top, and then—*Oh my*, Nanette thought, *whatever have I done?*

She felt so damn embarrassed, and there was no sign of James. She got up and took a long hot shower, dressed, and then discovered a note on the nightstand from James: *Thank you for a wonderful evening. Have early appointments and did not want to wake you. See you at the audition.*

Nanette felt her stomach tighten. She felt so very vulnerable, so very foolish. She wanted to call Devin, but how could she? She had betrayed him, that good and decent man. To tell him such a thing, such a mistake, would do no good.

She had the strongest desire to check out of the hotel, fly back to Florida—and what? Return to Devin as if nothing had happened? She couldn't play that part; she wanted no part of playing that part.

Give it time, she told herself. *This is the worst moment. Hopefully, things will become clear.* So she would prepare for the audition and allow her life drama to unfold.

CHAPTER 40

I T HAD BEEN TWO DAYS since Devin had received Nanette's message, and he had heard nothing since. He had finished shingling the shed roof and was now cutting and installing shelves, finishing up the job.

Last night, he'd had a crazy dream—he had flown to Los Angeles, only to discover that Nanette had married Manion.

"I'm sorry I didn't let you know, Devin," Nanette had said with an indifferent laugh as she threw a lascivious look at Manion, who had a condescending smirk on his face.

"You'd best get on back to where you came from, handyman," Manion had said with a dismissive wave. "She's mine—now and forever."

Devin had woken in a sweat, with beads of perspiration on his forehead. He had checked his alarm clock, which glowed three in the morning. He knew sleeping was not an option, so he lay in bed for two wide-eyed hours, as the dream kept cascading through his mind. Could something be going on between Nanette and her former high school beau? Could staying at the Beverly Hills Hotel, with all its charm, have cast a spell on Nanette that Manion had taken advantage of? Manion came across as a smooth operator, all outward charm, but inside, was there any substance, any character?

In the end, would Manion leave Nanette high and dry? Devin couldn't imagine that Manion had flown Nanette out to LA and put her up in such excellent living quarters, just to have a fling with his high school sweetheart—or could he?

As Devin secured the last shelf, he remembered the exchange of words between Nanette and him.

"Promise me one thing."

"Anything."

"You won't go on your way."

"I promise."

And if she had gone her way? What then?

CHAPTER 41

NANETTE WAS UP EARLY ON Wednesday morning, took a brisk walk around the hotel grounds, and then had a light breakfast of tea and a muffin at the Fountain Coffee Room in the hotel. She felt 100 percent better than when she had arisen yesterday. But her guilt in what she had allowed to take place with James still weighed heavily on her.

Even if Devin weren't in her life, she still would have been upset with herself for allowing it to happen. She thought about the actresses who had slept their way to stardom—some voluntarily; others most likely felt compelled. She hadn't felt compelled; more like letting the glitter of the moment get the best of her.

It did bother her that James had not reached out to her since that night. Nanette did see the irony that she had not contacted Devin either, but that was because she felt so darned ashamed. It was becoming clear that James was not to be trusted. *Duh.*

Even back in high school, James had been a smooth operator. Her best friend, who was dating a buddy of James, told Nanette that James was seeing a girl from another school. When Nanette had confronted James, he'd said it was someone he played doubles tennis with, and that it was all a lie.

He had been so sincere—and looking back now, overly so—that Nanette believed him, or at least that is what she told herself. And the other night, she had let herself fall into another of his traps. She remembered basking in a wine-induced haze in the glamour of Hollywood, where it was so easy to subconsciously alter one's persona.

Oh, how she wished she could go back in time and correct her foolishness. Nanette had acted like a wayward schoolgirl who had allowed herself to be charmed by her first love, who had showered her with attention.

Devin, on the other hand, was as honorable and trustworthy person as she could ask for. And what type of person was she for Devin? One who slept with her high school sweetheart on her first time away.

She needed to put all that aside, for she wanted to be at her best for the audition. After everything that had taken place, she still wanted an opportunity to perform before these Hollywood producers, to put her talent on display, not for any fame or fortune but because she considered herself an actress, and actresses act. She wasn't even sure, at this point, that she would accept the part, but she wanted to see this through.

After breakfast, she returned to her room and reviewed her lines, trying to get inside the head of her character, Julia. As she said the lines aloud, she thought about the pain a mother would feel at losing a child to a cult and how the heartache would show on her face, while maintaining a levelheadedness in trying to get her back.

Nanette decided to leave early for the audition, as James had told her that Sandra Sommers was auditioning before her.

Nanette slipped into the far back entrance to the Rodeo Ballroom. Sitting at the round table were Reggie and Barry and three staff members. Sandra was standing on stage with a young woman, auditioning. "Darling," Sandra said in a voice gripped with empathy, "you must believe that I care about you—that I want what is best for you."

Nanette was struck by the pure believability of the performance she was witnessing; at the same time, she asked herself, *Where is James?*

As Sandra continued her audition, hitting all the right emotional tones and stances, Reggie watched with casual interest, but Barry seemed to be listening to every word as if it was her last. His crossed forearms rested on the table; his head lifted forward and up toward the stage. He shot a look at Reggie, as if to say, *See? I told you.*

Nanette had to agree with Barry's silent rave review. Sandra Sommers was a formidable talent.

When Sandra finished, she came down off the stage, and Barry greeted her with a high-five.

One of the assistants at the table motioned Nanette to approach. As she came forward, she passed Sandra, who slid a glance Nanette's way but with no acknowledgement at all.

"Are you ready, Ms. Brinson?" Reggie said, appraising her.

"Yes," Nanette said. She headed for the stage—with James nowhere to be seen.

CHAPTER 42

B Y NOON, NANETTE WAS BACK at her room after the audition. She thought she had given it her best shot. She transformed her anger with James into controlled emotion. The fact that he didn't show his face or even contact her actually provided her a sense of freedom, a what-the-heck, go-for-it mentality. She sensed she had little chance for the role, so why not let it all out?

When she stepped down from the stage, one of the aides told her they would contact her with their decision within twenty-four hours. Reggie and Barry said not a word to her as she passed them; they sat next to each other, silently observing the female auditioner depart the premises. She had an idea as to what the decision would be.

Nanette sat on the side of her bed and felt a sudden fatigue wash over her. What an experience, not all of it bad, and a hard life lesson learned. She kicked off her slip-on shoes, put her feet up on the bed, and laced her fingers behind her neck. Never in her life had Nanette felt so alone. The magic of the hotel, the city of Beverly Hills, and the allure of Hollywood no longer seemed so desirable.

What did seem desirable was a fella back in Pleasantville. She needed to figure out a way of telling Devin what had occurred without losing him. How she would pull that off, she had not a clue.

She decided to call room service—she was still on James's dime and might as well enjoy it. She ordered the salmon and avocado Caesar salad, which made her think of the grand times she and Devin had enjoyed when he grilled salmon on her patio.

When her food arrived, she had already changed into her bathing suit and shirt. She went out to the bungalow pool to the same table as before. There wasn't a soul at the pool, which seemed appropriate for her present state of mind. She dug into the salad, which was good, but she liked Devin's grilled salmon better.

She wanted to talk to Devin but had an idea that involved waiting until she got word about her audition. She sent him a text: "Had second audition this morning. Will know in twenty-four hours. Call when I find out."

Nanette finished her salad, removed her shirt, and stretched out in a lounge chair. Across the pool, she spotted Sandra Sommers, in a blood-red bikini, dropping a tote bag next to a lounge chair and sitting down. She looked absolutely stunning and every bit the part of a Hollywood starlet—the killer body with curves and bulges in all the right places—and more than that, she carried herself with a calm confidence.

Sandra looked across the pool, saw Nanette, and lifted her hand, a knowing smile of recognition emerging across her face. She got up and walked over. "Hello, there. I believe we are competing for the same part."

Nanette's mouth dropped open before she regained her poise. "Hi." She offered her hand to the chair next to her. "Would you like to sit?"

Sandra eased into the lounge chair, her long legs, which looked to have been formed on a lathe, stretched out. "I thought I knew all my competition in this town." Her lush brown eyes brightened in a questioning glint.

"I flew out for the audition," Nanette said.

"Sandra Sommers here." She extended her hand, which Nanette shook.

"Nanette Brinson. Nice to meet you."

"Let me guess," Sandra said. "James Manion was your sponsor." She threw Nanette a look that said, *Am I right?*

Nanette got a chime for a text and thought it must be Devin responding. She lifted her finger to Sandra, indicating one moment. The text was not from Devin but James:

Sorry to say Sandra Sommers got the part. Am at the airport, flying to San Fran—great seeing you. Had to cut short your stay at hotel. Check out tomorrow. Regards, James.

Nanette felt her jaw drop. *Huh?* She sank back in her chair and felt as though she would die right there. "I'm sorry," Nanette said. "Yes, that was him, telling me you got the part."

"Really?" Sandra said. Her phone chimed, and she reached in her tote bag and read her text. "Well, I'll be. That was Barry, confirming."

"You are a very fine actress," Nanette said. "You deserved the part."

"As are you," Sandra said. "I watched both your auditions."

They got to talking, and Nanette told Sandra about her relationship with James in high school, the reunion, and his showing up in Pleasantville for her play.

"Whoever he was in high school," Sandra said in a cool, observational tone, "he's not that guy anymore—but I'm guessing you know that by now." Sandra went on to say that James had a nickname in the business; he was known as the little prick. "And I mean that both figuratively and literally," she added.

Nanette felt a comfort level in talking with Sandra—two women performing in a world controlled by men. "I made a big mistake the other night with James," she said. She looked over at Sandra to gauge her interest.

"Get in line," Sandra said. "He wined and dined me years ago, and I gave it up for him." A smirk split her face. "I never heard from him again about a part he had told me I'd be perfect for. I learned my lesson and decided to use my assets." She swept her hand in front of her bosom and down her legs. "I let Barry have his way with me to help get this part, and after it's in the can, I will drop him like the sleazy scumbag he is. I call it sleeping with the enemy."

Nanette then told Sandra about Devin and the situation she was in.

"'To err is human; to forgive, divine.' Tell him the truth, and if he doesn't accept your apology, then move on." Sandra brought her leg up and placed her hand atop her knee. "But if he does, then you have found yourself a keeper."

CHAPTER 43

AFTER FINISHING THE SHED, DEVIN decided to take the rest of the week off and start his next job on Monday. Early Wednesday morning, he took a long bike ride around the park and then into the interior trails. His hybrid bike was solid in traversing the sometimes-bumpy terrain.

Emerging from the interior, he stopped at a spot where he and Nanette always watched the wildlife. It provided a full view of the lake, rimmed by the foliage of bald cypress, gumbo limbo, and a variety of oak and maple trees. The morning mist was rising from the light blue water as the sun lifted above the tree line, its warm light taking over the day.

Devin looked for beavers, one in particular that he had named Muncho for its penchant for eating plants on the shoreline. But the only wildlife he saw was a mallard paddling along the shore, rasping out a one-two call, and then another, as though possibly in search of a mate. Its head was glossy green, and its wings and belly were tipped gray, indicating the male of the species. The bird flapped its wings and scooted over the water before lifting up and flying off. Devin watched until the bird disappeared into the horizon. "Good luck finding her," Devin said to the vanished bird.

After a shower and a late lunch, Devin took a nap on the back deck in an Adirondack chair. When he awoke, he saw that a message from Nanette had arrived.

He decided against responding. *Let her wait this time.* It wasn't that he was mad at her, more perplexed. Yes, he still wanted to be with her, but he couldn't keep responding to every text like her lapdog.

Whatever way it went with Nanette, he thought he could deal with it. If she were going to break it off, then he would work his way out of the pain and go on with his life—at least, that's what he told himself. If she still wanted to see him, then great, but he'd like an answer to the cryptic way she was contacting him. Bits and pieces of information about her stay in California without any substance. What was that all about?

And if something had gone on with Manion, first off, would she tell him? And second, if she did, how would he respond?

He knew he was once again overthinking the situation, and possibly his imagination was getting the best of him, but Devin did not think so. He trusted his gut, and his gut told himself something had transpired, and Manion was the likely culprit.

Devin's intuition had been an asset all of his adult life, starting in Vietnam, when, in the middle of his tour, he arrived at Bao Loc in the central highlands to begin construction of solid-steel matting for a C-130 runway. His platoon arrived by bus in the middle of the night with no lights on, so as not to alert the enemy.

The construction was to begin at sunrise, but first, Devin insisted to the commanding base officer that a security sweep be done of the surrounding jungle. Viet Cong could easily hide in thick foliage, and for the first time, his gut had spoken to him—beware of the jungle.

A recon team of six performed a cursory sweep, and they returned with the all-*clear.* Not satisfied, Devin had his men build a trench bunker, supported by sandbags, that they could quickly get to in case of attack. They began construction of the runway, but Devin told his men to keep alert. "That jungle is a danger."

Sure enough, two days in, while Devin and his crew were laying the first steel matting, they came under heavy machine-gun fire from the jungle. They hustled into their bunker; fortunately, no one was hit. Ever since that day, Devin had trusted his instincts.

And if he could withstand the pressure of staying vigilant every day in Vietnam for a year, while building in the most inhospitable conditions, and come out of it in one piece, he decided he could survive the unknown in regard to his status with Nanette Brinson.

CHAPTER 44

EARLY FRIDAY MORNING, NANETTE TOOK a cab from the hotel to LAX. En route, she pondered a few things. She had not heard back from Devin. Had he had enough of her thoughtlessness? Looking back from his vantage point, she saw clearly how poorly she had handled the entire situation, other than giving her audition her best.

She decided that she would call Devin when she arrived at her house. She didn't want to talk to him over the phone but in person. She would take Sandra's advice and tell Devin the truth, everything—that is, if he gave her the opportunity. And even if he did, she couldn't blame him if he told her that he was done with her after she told him about James, whom Sandra so aptly described as the little prick.

Sandra was a survivor, but listening to her and seeing who she had become—a tough, pragmatic woman who used her physical beauty as a tool in her career—was a cautionary warning about the pitfalls of life as an actress in Hollywood. It was a life Nanette wanted no part of.

Even if she had been offered the part, after all that occurred, she would not have accepted. She wanted nothing to do with any project that James and his fellow scumbags—as Sandra, once again, had so aptly described—had anything to do with. Beyond that, not that it was going to happen, but Nanette was no longer interested in a film career. Local theater was more to her liking, allowing the thespian in her to perform on stage.

A taxi dropped off Nanette at her house. After unpacking, she took a seat at the kitchen nook. She started to call Devin but stopped, as her heart clocking in her throat. The moment was upon her, the moment where the remainder of the course of her life would be determined.

Nanette realized that what she had with Devin was special—a relationship that she may well have thrown away. What had she been thinking when she'd spent the night with James? Who was that woman who allowed the glitter and glamour of Beverly Hills and that smooth-talking James to blow up everything she had built with Devin? Whoever she had allowed herself to be in Beverly Hills, she no longer was.

Nanette took a deep breath and phoned Devin. After six rings, his voice mail came on: "Hi, this is Devin. Sorry I missed your call. Please leave your name and number, and I will get back to you."

Nanette froze. She regained a semblance of poise. "Hello, Devin. I just got home. Would like to see you and talk. Call me when you get a chance."

Nanette heard the tension in her voice, the anxious bleat. The shoe was now on the other foot, a situation for which she was entirely responsible.

CHAPTER 45

EVIN SPENT HIS OFF DAY puttering in the yard. He weeded the backyard, mowed the grass, and then weeded some in front before heading out for a long, lazy bike ride in Seminole Park, where he saw Muncho submerging in and then coming out of the water—such a carefree life that aquatic creature seemed to live.

Back home, he took a shower and dressed in T-shirt and shorts, grabbed a beer from the fridge, and went out to the back deck. He checked his phone, which he had forgotten to take on his ride, and saw that Nanette had called.

"Huh. Well, I'll be," he said aloud. He listened to her message. He could hear tension in her voice when she said, "Would like to see you and talk." Something was up. In the last few days, in the silence, their relationship had entered an unknown territory. Why that was, Devin was unsure. He had his ideas, but that's all they were. But in hearing the quiver in her voice, his gut told him that revelation was in the air.

Devin called Nanette, and she answered on the first ring.

"Hello, Devin," she said in a happy voice. But behind the glee, there remained a trace of nerves.

"Good to finally hear your voice," Devin said. He wanted to ask about the audition, but something told him to hold up.

"Can you come over?" Nanette said, her tone straightforward.

"Twenty minutes?"

"Perfect."

Devin didn't bother to ask if they should plan on drinks and dinner. No, it seemed that whatever came out of their *talk* would determine whether there were any more drinks and dinner.

CHAPTER 46

AFTER SPEAKING TO DEVIN, NANETTE went into her bedroom and changed out of her travel wardrobe of a blouse and skirt and into shorts and a T-shirt. She wanted to be as comfortable as possible. She checked herself in the mirror and noted that her time spent under the benevolent California sun at the bungalow pool had given her face a honey-gold glow. She was a young-looking older woman who had a young-looking older man coming over to discuss—what, exactly? The chime of the doorbell broke her thought.

Nanette opened the front door, and there he stood, tall, ruggedly handsome, and with a quiet grace about him that she just noticed. "Hi," Nanette said with as much of an upbeat tone as she could muster. "Shall we sit out back?" She offered her hand for him to enter.

"Sure," Devin said as he stepped inside.

They walked silently out back, as it seemed they both realized a *moment* was about to happen. After they sat, Nanette forced a smile across the table.

"I take it that you have something of consequence to tell me," Devin said.

Nanette took a *here-goes* breath. "I made a big mistake in California." She looked directly at Devin. "I spent the night with James."

Devin squinted in an appraising manner at the raised beds he had built with such painstaking care. His expression was wounded, but the gaze was steadfast for what seemed an eternity before he nodded calmly, as though he had come to a decision. He turned his attention back to Nanette. "And?"

"I want to tell you how sorry I am. That I realized now what a foolish thing I did. If you never want to see me again—"

"Are you done with Manion?" Devin cut in.

"Yes," Nanette said; she felt her voice cracking. "And I'm done with Hollywood and only want you back in my life. Can you forgive me?" Nanette felt an avalanche of tears streaking her cheeks.

"The exchange of words we had about getting to know each other and not going on our way—I like to think of it as our promise to each other."

"Yes," Nanette choked out. "I like to think that too."

"Well," Devin said, "you did go on your way, but you came back to me." He took a breath, with a glint of moisture in his eyes. "I can't imagine living without you in this life. I love you, Nanette." Devin reached for Nanette's hand and laced her fingers through his. "Let us put what happened in California behind us."

Nanette felt her heart swoon as she remembered Sandra's words at the pool. She had herself a keeper.

Printed in the United States
by Baker & Taylor Publisher Services